THE YANKEE PRESENT

Philip Ross Chadwick

Author's Tranquility Press
MARIETTA, GEORGIA

Copyright © 2021 by **Philip Ross Chadwick**

All rights reserved. No part of this publication may be reproduced, distributed or transmitted in any form or by any means, without prior written permission.

Philip Ross Chadwick/Author's Tranquility Press
2706 Station Club Drive SW
Marietta, GA 30060
www.authorstranquilitypress.com

Publisher's Note: This is a work of fiction. Names, characters, places, and incidents are a product of the author's imagination. Locales and public names are sometimes used for atmospheric purposes. Any resemblance to actual people, living or dead, or to businesses, companies, events, institutions, or locales is completely coincidental.

Philip Ross Chadwick/ The Yankee Present
Paperback   ISBN: 978-1-957208-16-9
EBook   ISBN: 978-1-957208-17-6

Dedication

*This book was written in memory of my wife Gladena (Dee) Chadwick.
Her encouragement gave the incentive for the completion of the project.*

Contents

Chapter 1 1

Chapter 2 17

Chapter 3 27

Chapter 4 34

Chapter 5 40

Chapter 6 48

Chapter 7 52

Chapter 8 55

Chapter 9 70

Chapter 10 74

Chapter 11 91

Chapter 12 99

Chapter 13 109

Chapter 14 117

Chapter 15 123

Chapter 16 129

Chapter 17 136

Chapter 18 142

Chapter 19 153

Chapter 20 159

Chapter 21 165

Chapter 22 169

Chapter 23 175

Chapter 24 181

Chapter 25 186

Chapter 26 195

Chapter 27 200

Chapter 28 205

Chapter 29 217

Chapter 30 221

Chapter 31 225

Chapter 1

Whether it was the snort or the gushing warm air from the horse's nostrils, Thomas was uncertain what brought him back to the present. As he lay on his back on the cold ground, he gradually returned to his senses. When his eyes finally opened, he looked up to the night sky, and the fuzzy points of light coalesced into stars. A turn of his head brought into view a full moon partially covered by clouds.

He suddenly became aware of a tremendous pain in his left side. He slowly moved his right hand across his chest and felt the tattered hole in his coat. Pushing his fingers inside, he was aware of ripped flesh. Withdrawing his fingers, they felt sticky. He brought his fingertips to his nostrils and smelled blood. It was an unmistakable odor he had smelled many times in the past few months. He had smelled animal blood from the hog killings on the farm and the animals he had hunted, but this blood smelled different. It was his.

The horse lowered its head and snorted again. Thomas tried to reach up, but his hand fell onto his chest. Exhaustion took over. He fell out of consciousness and into the blackness of night.

"That was too close!" someone yelled as dirt fell like rain.

The explosion has occurred just a few yards beyond the rail fence that provided cover for the line of troops. Their captain had ordered the group of men to which Thomas was assigned to spread out along the western flank. What had started out as a skirmish had turned into a full-fledged battle.

The Federal infantry had changed tactics from worrisome sniper fire to charges across the open field with artillery providing support. Since the Confederates held the high ground, the Federals were at a disadvantage.

The Confederates had successfully defended each attack. Action of the Federals had only caused a slowdown of the work the Confederates were undertaking. With a quick exchange of rifles for their work tools, the Confederates were ready to defend their position.

The blast from the cannon caused Thomas to creep closer to the fence to take a closer look at the Federal line.

Word among the Confederates was that they were facing McClelland and his army of twenty-five thousand or more soldiers supported by five artillery batteries. The artillery was stationed a thousand yards behind the infantry line. The artillery commander was firing right to left upon the Confederate defenses.

The Confederate army consisted of eighteen thousand soldiers and three artillery batteries. The Confederates, however, held the advantage as the Federals had to cover the open ground by running uphill across a meadow.

The meadow put distance between the armies from where Thomas lay. For three days, both armies had been intent on completing their objective. Most of the Confederate divisions were deployed on the north side of the Chickahominy River to keep McClelland from crossing, thus allowing the Federals to divide the units of the Army of Virginia. The rest of the divisions tried securing the crossing points of the river.

As Thomas peered through the rails of the fence, he saw the field before him strewn with fallen blue-clad bodies. It had been a standoff for the two previous days. The Federals had charged the Southern line once each day. Each time, the Southern boys cut them down.

Apparently, the Federals were tiring of the stalemate. Twice that day, they had made a charge, and twice the rebel yell had gone up at their retreat among a forest of white oaks. At least those Federals had shade from the sun. The rest of the Federal line could only fall back out of range to breastworks that had been established on the open field. The Federals had tried four times - and had failed four times- to overrun the Confederates during the three-day confrontation, and each time, the Southern army had successfully repulsed them.

Rumor along the Southern line was that McClelland might be waiting for additional units. Then again, as some speculated, it was the timorous nature of the Union general to be less than forceful in carrying out battle plans. Perhaps the strength of the rebel force was not known- and the objective was keep the Confederate division busy while other Federal units were spreading out over northern Virginia. The plan of attack had cost him many of his forces as they still occupied the field under the afternoon sun.

The Confederate army, which was part of the Stonewall Brigade, enjoyed the shade of cottonwoods and sycamores and the cool breeze coming from the river behind them. The rest of the time, the two sides had settled for taking sniper shots at anything that moved. The sporadic rifle fire was just annoying enough to keep everyone on edge and to keep needed sleep from happening.

When the wind changed direction, the Confederates were reminded of the carnage that had taken place. Thomas noted the smell was worse than when he cleaned the barn stalls after the winter. Decaying human flesh had an odor that was different from animal excrement.

Looking through the rails and a cloud of smoke, Thomas strained to see where the blast had been launched from. He was startled to see a line of Federals leap from the cover of their fortifications and start out across the meadow. "Here they come again " he shouted as he grabbed his rifle.

Placing a cap under the hammer, he shouldered his rifle and pointed. As his finger tightened around the trigger, he heard the hammer click and felt the jolt of the exploding powder. He was the first to get off a shot. Though he had not taken direct aim on any one particular invader, he saw a Yankee fall. He saw the surprised look and anguish of pain as his bullet found its mark.

Thomas was stunned at the sight. To his knowledge, this was the first man he had killed. He had fired his rifle many times but had never seen the result. He was the first to fire, and the enemy lay still as the oncoming horde streamed past the fallen body.

The only things Thomas had ever killed were hogs and squirrels on the farm. Somebody now lay dead. Who was he? Where was he from? What about his family? For a moment, the image of a lady captured his being. It wasn't Jenny, but tears were streaming down her cheeks. Thomas thought it was the wife of the man he had slain.

The image took Thomas from the war raging in front of him. Did his victim live on a farm like him? How many children had he made fatherless? A hollow feeling creeped through Thomas as he stared at his deed. However, this was war as he was suddenly reminded when a Yankee bullet struck the rail in front of him and splinters filled the air. Ducking for cover, he began the methodical ritual of reloading.

The Confederates sent a hail of bullets toward the charging Yankees. Dozens fell after the first volley, but onward they came. The second line of Confederates stepped up and unleashed their fury of death while the first line reloaded. A third blast of rifle fire sent the Yankees scurrying back to the woods, and the Confederates congratulated themselves with yells and waves of their caps. They had repulsed the enemy once again. Fresh cries of pain from the wounded were now heard, and Thomas knew that the stench from the dead would only get stronger. He tried to erase from his mind the look on the face of the one he had shot. He wondered what hot lead felt like as it pierced the body. He rolled to his back and pulled his kepi down over his eyes to block the afternoon sun. The cries and moans of the wounded filled his ears.

Night eventually arrived, and Thomas and the others had to settle for cold rations again. Any fires could give away the position of the Confederate line. The Federals would use the firelight as targets for their snipers, and with any luck, they might pick off a secesh.

It became Thomas's turn to take picket duty. As he walked the line, his thoughts reviewed the day. The cruel war had now made its way into his soul. He could still see the look of pain on the face of the man he had sent to his eternal resting place.

The hollow feeling completely engulfed him. Each step jarred the moment only deeper into his thoughts. The war now had such an unimaginable grip that his picket steps became rote. He stared straight ahead, not giving full attention to the duty.

Thomas found himself reliving the spring day he and others from Lone Oak and Palmyra, Tennessee, had reported to go to Camp Duncan just north of Clarksville. Colonel W. A. Quarrels had sworn them in on the train depot platform.

He had seen men leave Clarksville before. He had seen the tears on the faces of the mothers, the wives, the sweethearts, and other loved ones. He had heard the music of the band. He had even been a part of the cheering and shouting as volunteers boarded the train to face the invading Yankees. He now realized if all those events were supposed to make the soldiers feel better as they traveled into the unknown, it had not had that effect on him.

He began to recall the faces of his loved ones. He saw the grim look on Pa's face as they shook hands and embraced. Ma tried to maintain a smile on her face, but she let a tear escape as their hug ended. Almeda's tears dampened his cheeks as they had clung to each other for the moment.

Thomas maintained his composure fairly well until it was time to say goodbye to Samuel. Samuel had not been able to look him in the eye, and the shaking of his head had the message of "don't go." As they wrapped each other in their arms, Samuel buried his face into his shoulder and said, "I love you, brother." Thomas closed his eyes, trying to hold back tears.

Finally, it came time to say goodbye to Jenny. For a moment, they simply stood looking at each other. Thomas studied her face as if trying to burn a picture of her into his memory. He placed his hands on the sides of her head and looked at her golden hair parted in the middle, producing two long braids tied off with lace ribbons she had crocheted herself. He grasped each braid, gently tugged on them, and then folded his hands around her cheeks. He pulled her face toward him and lightly kissed her forehead. With a finger, he followed her nose down to her quivering lips. He looked intently into her blue eyes, which had left a stream of tears on each cheek.

He put his arms around her slender waist and pulled her closer.

Jenny put her arms around his neck and buried her face in his chest.

For a moment, Thomas wished he was not leaving.

Jenny whispered, "I love you, my darling. I don't want you to go, but I know you are doing what you think is right."

Thomas held on tightly and said, "I love you so very, very much. Most families have sent at least one, and some families have sent two loved ones to war. I must represent our family for the cause. Everyone says the war will not last long, so I should not be gone long. Don't worry about me."

"Board the train, soldiers." The call from Colonel Quarrels shortened their embrace.

With one last "I love you," Thomas released his hold on her. The embrace seemed way too short.

He rushed to board the train passenger car and get a window seat. Lowering the window, he pushed his head and arms through the opening to see his family for as long as possible. They exchanged goodbyes as the train began to move out of the station. Waving with both arms, he watched those on the platform grow smaller as the train put distance between him and his loved ones.

When he could no longer see the station, he lowered himself into his seat. Apprehension about things to come had filled his mind, and the clacking sounds of the rails quickened as the train gathered speed. He had never been on a train before, and the experience was exciting. He stood up to get a look at the quickly passing landscape.

Thomas remembered getting dizzy from trying to keep up with the swift passing objects outside the window. The train was going much faster than any buggy ride he had experienced. Feeling lightheaded, he slid down in the seat. He closed his eyes and wrapped his arms around himself.

The swaying rail car took him back to the previous night. He remembered being held by

Jenny after their romantic interlude. He had brushed tears from her cheek with a lock of her hair. No words would console Jenny. She had held him so tight that it was suffocating. Sleep eventually had come to them, and the morning had come way too soon.

Thomas's thoughts were interrupted by the passenger next to him. "My name is William Harris, but you can call me Will." He extended his hand.

Thomas took the hand, revealed who he was, and the two began a conversation that would seal a friendship for the months to come.

After a while, they settled in for the ride to their assignment. Thomas slipped back into thoughts about home. Would he ever see home again? Would Samuel be able to help Pa carry out all the farmwork? His biggest worry was Jenny. Her family was close by, but he was concerned about her.

The slowing train interrupted the somber moment. He pulled his watch from his pocket. They had left Clarksville about a half hour ago. Thomas sat up and looked out the window at a field covered with rows of white tents.

"This must be Camp Duncan," Will said. Thomas nodded.

There was smoke coming from campfires. On one side of the field, men were marching in close order with their rifles.

"That'll be us tomorrow," someone said as they began to exit the train car.

Even before they were out, someone else was yelling directions. The unearthly sounds were coming from a short, bad – tempered Irishman. The orders and swearing came from between teeth still clenched around a short pipe stem. "My name is Captain O'Reilly to you worthless examples of excrement. Me job is to make soldiers outta ye simpletons. I suspect some of ye don't know ye right foot from ye left. But that'll change by the time I gits through wid of ye. I've been a soldier in the army longer than some of yours has been alive. I've marched to Texas an' back, and I come here to teach ye how to be soldiers. Some of ye I see look like you can put in a full day of work." He paused and looked over the rim of his glasses. His eyes narrowed as they surveyed the soldiers. "Some of ye look a bit lazy, but I intend to get a day's full of work outta ye delicate laddies."

Thomas was taken aback by the demeanor of the bearded officer. He stood frozen and wide-eyed as more insults were hurled to the assembly.

From somewhere near the back, someone shouted, "We'll show you what kind of soldiers us Tennessee boys will make, Stumpy."

The Irishman immediately began to shove bodies aside as he made his way through the crowd. "Who said that? If'n I find out which one o' you blokes said that, ye wont'en be alikin' it."

Thomas wanted to turn around to see who was being addressed, but he remembered the words of Harold Edwards, who ran the Lone Oak general store and had served in Texas: "Eyes front always."

When O'Reilly made his way back to the front of the group, his face was even redder than before. It took a moment for him to gather himself. "There's supposed to be forty of ye. Gimme four volunteers and line up behind them now."

The shuffling of feet and jostling of bodies began immediately

Thomas found himself pushed to the front of one of the lines. With hands behind his slightly bent back, O'Reilly began an inspection of his charges. Silence settled over the group until O'Reilly reached the back row. "I said four even lines. Why's this line got two extra bodies- and this line is short?"

For a moment, there was silence. "I said why?"

A feeble voice announced, "We three is buddies."

"Buddies?" exclaimed O'Reilly. "Buddies, when an order is given, you ain't got no buddies."

Thomas could only imagine what was taking place behind him.

O'Reilly appeared momentarily to face the group again. "When I give the order to march, start off with ye left foot. We'll march across the field to our tents. Does anybody not know which is ye left foot?" After a brief pause and with a bit of footwork, which the new recruits would soon learn, O'Reilly turned and shouted, "Now march."

The person behind Thomas stepped on his heel, causing him to stumble, but he was able to recover before O'Reilly turned around.

They walked past a formation of men being instructed how to wheel right and wheel left. The rows of tents reminded Thomas of walking down a street in Clarksville.

O'Reilly eventually gave the command to halt, but some of the men at the rear did not hear and kept marching. Some stumbled, and some fell, knocking others to the ground.

O'Reilly was incensed. More shouts and oaths were offered. Thomas was sure if he had access to a cane or stick, some of those laughing would have been the recipients of a blow of the Irishman's temper.

When order was restored, the tent assignments were given.

Thomas found himself in a group of seven strangers. He unrolled his new blanket, placed his rifle and hat on it, and left the tent.

They were ordered to form up for a walk to the kitchen tent.

Thomas suddenly felt the pangs of hunger. It was mid-afternoon, and it had been several hours since they had gathered at the farm for his last breakfast. He eagerly awaited the offerings of those doing the cooking. What he received on his plate was nothing like what Ma had ever made. "What is this?"

"We've got us another mamma's boy," announced the scraggly figure behind the kettle. "Did you never hear of skilligalee? You will have it in the morning again – only then it will be fried."

Thomas would learn that most of the cooks had been removed from their units because they could not keep up with marching maneuvers or did not pass inspection and caused their unit to fail. He would soon realize the camp meals would be quite different from the meals Ma prepared.

Thomas stopped in his tracks and realized he was not walking the picket line. He shouldered his rifle and resumed the methodical and monotonous steps. For a moment, he wondered which side was correct. He had heard the debates of his grandfather, father, and the other men of the community back home. As their words began to ring in his ears his faith in the Southern way was renewed, and he resolved to do all in his power to keep the cause alive.

Chapter 2

Thomas finished his hour of picket duty and prepared to sleep the rest of the night. He sat down against a tree and covered himself with his blanket. He was awakened by someone kicking his foot. He could not determine how long he had been asleep.

"What are you doing?" Thomas threw off his blanket and scrambled to his feet.

"What's your name," an officer said.

"I am sorry, sir." He stiffened and gave a salute. "My name is Thomas Lyle."

The officer said, "General A. P. Hill is ordering a special detail. I am to pick someone to lead fifteen men. I guess you are able enough. You are to advance two hundred yards farther to the west. Report any flanking movement that occurs and engage if necessary"

The officer turned and disappeared into the darkness of the night.

Thomas awoke the fifteen men pretty much in the same way his sleep had been interrupted. "We are to advance two hundred yards westward to observe any flanking movement by the Yankees."

Quietly and using the trees as cover, the detail moved forward for what Thomas thought was the required distance. They stationed themselves behind a rock outcrop and tree laps that had provided timbers for the Confederate works. A new picket order was established, and Thomas settled down for much- needed sleep.

The morning's stillness was shattered by two artillery blasts from cannons. The ground shook and woke Thomas from his nap. As he tried to clear his mind from the cobwebs of sleep, he crawled behind the rock outcrop.

The sunlight filtered through the limbs of the trees, illuminated the morning fog. The smoke drifted across the small clearing toward them. As the acrid smoke drifted around Thomas and his group, any remnants of sleep were erased.

Two Federal Mountain howitzers had been placed for what he calculated was less than seventy or eighty yards from where they were stationed. From the way they were positioned, the cannons could fire upon a portion of the

Confederate line. If the Federals could weaken part of the Southern line, then they could overtake much of the Confederate position. There was a small contingent of infantry with the artillery for support.

It only took a few moments for the others to join Thomas. "The Federals set those up last night," someone said.

Thomas knew the howitzers had been dismantled and brought to the position. The pieces of the smaller artillery guns could be carried by soldiers and reassembled without the noise of mules or rolling caisson wheels.

"Yeah ... because we ain't been fired on from there before."

"Not on my watch."

"It doesn't matter on whose watch it occurred," said Thomas. "It's been done, and we have got to do something about it. If they take out this western part of the line, we can be out-flanked-and they will capture all of General Hill's army on this side of the river.

From their hiding place, Thomas and the group had a clear line of sight. The artillery commander was preparing to unleash another barrage of fire. Luckily the cannons were wedged be- tween some trees and could not be easily shifted in the direction of where Thomas and his companions.

Thomas said, "We can't be touched by cannon fire, but how much rifle fire can we sustain? When we unload on them with our first rounds, they may hit us pretty hard with return fire."

"Do they even know we are here?" someone whispered.

"They must not," Thomas replied, "but they will after our first shot. Let's see if we can catch them off guard in the middle of their loading. Let's all fire at once and take out as many as possible. We won't be able to surprise them again."

The men prepared their weapons and waited for Thomas's signal.

Thomas watched the crew from each cannon as they made ready to fire. Just before the torch touched the vent hole, Thomas shouted, "Now!"

The little group of Confederates cut loose on those manning the cannons. Several fell, and the look on the faces of those still standing was one of surprise. It was apparent that the Federals did not know the two groups were so close.

The Confederates immediately began to take fire. The cannoneers who fell were replaced quickly and continued firing.

Other Federals began firing on Thomas and the group. A heated exchange of fire kept both sides busy. Thomas observed that some of the replacements were not from an artillery unit. Their lack of experience slowed the firing process, but when they did manage to load and fire, it brought havoc to the Confederate forces.

To save the Confederate line, Thomas's group would have to lay down a stiff blanket of fire. Both sides unleashed a furious exchange of lead. Along with the din of constant rifle fire, the percussion waves from the cannon blasts buffeted the small band of Confederates.

The fighting progressed for some time, and Thomas heard someone shouting. As he turned to get a better look, he was astonished to see a figure riding toward them.

The rider approached their position and waved his cap. "Give it to them, boys, and send them back north one way or another." The rider turned and rode back toward the main line zigzagging between the trees. Thomas could not decide if the rider was crazy or just plain drunk. The horse and rider eventually disappeared into the trees.

After almost an hour of intense fighting, the Confederates were holding their position, but the Federal cannons had put some holes in the Confederate line. Thomas's group had suffered only two wounded, but a major problem was creeping up on them. Their ammunition was getting low. If they did not keep the Federals at bay, the cannons would have free rein to cause heavy causalities on the main line.

"We can't run out of ammunition," Thomas exclaimed. "I am going to make a run to the supply wagons."

"You will never make it."

"I've got to," Thomas said. "If we don't keep them pinned down as much as possible, the cannons will slowly take out our line on this side of the river. Their infantry could sweep our end and move on our weakened defenses. Most of our army is on this side of the river. A loss on this side of the river would allow the Federals to overrun our remaining forces on the other side and move deeper into Virginia."

Thomas put down his rifle and ran toward the main column.

The Federal force saw him, and he began taking fire. More than once, bullets hit the tree he was hiding behind, splattering him with bark and splinters.

It seemed like he had run for miles as he sought the biggest trees for cover, yet his trip only took him the yardage he had put down in carrying out the order. He eventually reached the main body of Confederates and was no longer the main target. He began to look for a supply wagon. Thomas asked an officer for the location of the supply wagons.

"Who are you-and why are you needing ordnance?"

"I am Thomas Lyle of the Tennessee Fourteenth. I am in charge of a detail that was sent farther down the line to guard our left flank. We have received no supplies because of our position."

"Oh, you are the group opposite the Federal cannons that have flanked us." The officer pointed in the direction from which Thomas had come. "You men are keeping the pressure from those cannons to a minimum on our line here. All of the supply wagons have been moved back across the river for safety. You will have to cross one of the bridges to get to them. You and your men have been a big part of our battle. Great job." The officer extended a hand for Thomas to shake.

After releasing the grip of the officer, Thomas offered a salute, which the officer returned.

The officer pointed Thomas in the direction of the closest bridge. A corporal was assigned to escort Thomas to the bridge and to tell the guard to allow Thomas to pass.

Thomas found a wagon and pulled a box from beneath the canvas. He pried the top up and found shot, powder, and caps. He wondered if he was supposed to have an order to remove the much-needed ordnance. A supply officer had always issued their supplies before, but none was present. However, this was an emergency.

The box was heavy, and its size made it hard to carry, but Thomas was able to get the box to his shoulder. He began the trip back to the front line. He crossed the bridge and turned toward the left flank. Eventually, Thomas found himself in range of the troublesome Federal contingent. Thomas heard several cannon blasts and knew the casualties were mounting.

Thomas finally reached the point where he had to be cautious in his movements to avoid rifle fire. There were no trees that were large enough to hide himself and the box he was carrying. Thomas placed the box on the ground, crawled forward, and pushed the box of Federal presents. He did not want a Federal bullet to find its mark on the box. He sought the cover of tree stumps and rock out crops. He crawled along a shallow ditch, but the box frequently bumped into rocks, which slowed his progress. At last, he made his way back to the rock outcrop where he had left his rifle. The group was loading the last of the ammunition.

Thomas and the group began an unrelenting volley of fire. Several of the artillery company had been taken out, and his detail suffered two killed and four wounded. Two of the wounded were not serious enough to prevent them from fighting. An occasional blast from the cannons further weakened the Confederate line.

If only there was some way to knock out the cannons, thought Thomas.

As Thomas watched the loading preparations, he had an idea. As the charge was being taken out of the enemy's limber box-and the lid was still up-Thomas took aim on the powder charge. In an instant, his idea was answered.

The first explosion of the powder charges the cannoneer was holding set off the remaining charges in the limber box. The blast blew men, ground, and all manner of debris skyward. When the smoke cleared, both cannons had been knocked from their frames and were out of commission.

The explosion garnered the attention of the Confederate line, and they sent up a cheer. The cannons were now useless, and no Federals had escaped the blast. Thomas and his group could relax somewhat, but they kept a vigilant watch for any other flanking movements.

The afternoon sun drenched the open field with unbearable heat for the wounded men. Several times, the Federal companies had mounted a charge, and each time, the Confederates had driven them back. Thomas knew there were many new bodies on the field. He positioned himself to see the open space between the battle lines. He could see movement from some, but most were eerily still. The contortions of their bodies would be most uncomfortable if life was still within.

For a moment, Thomas felt sorry for them. He heard someone cry out for water. Thomas reached for his canteen and would have offered a drink to the poor soul if it was not a war. Thomas was thirsty, but he decided not to pull the plug for even a small slip. As the reality of war settled in, his compassion faded. He realized that one of the enemy's bullets could have had his name on it. He shivered at the thought and offered up a prayer of thanks for his safety. He longed for a chance to sleep.

Chapter 3

As daylight was waning, the Federals made one more assault. Again, the Confederates repulsed the advance, inflicting heavy losses on their foe. The Federals realized they could not pull a flanking maneuver. As the Confederates held the higher ground, it became apparent that a frontal assault would not be successful either. The battle gradually subsided, and it was as if the Federals simply melted back into the woods or behind the breastworks.

A rider carrying a white flag soon began to make his way across the body strewn field. The rider cautiously picked a path so the horse would not step on the fallen or wounded. The Confederates answered by sending out a contingent to meet the flag of truce. After a brief encounter, the riders parted and returned to their respective lines.

The battlefield was soon busy with stretcher bearers and ambulances picking up the Federal wounded and dead. As darkness fell, the lights from the bobbing lanterns reminded Thomas of lightning bugs over the hayfield in front of his cabin.

As Thomas sat against a log with a small fire before him, even a meal of hardtack and what was called "coffee" tasted good. It had been a long day, and Thomas was spent both physic- ally and mentally.

It took some time, but the Federals removed their dead and wounded. The Confederates watched as their adversaries loaded their wagons. The air was full of shouts of those loading the things that were worth picking up. The neighs of the mules and shouts of the drivers told Thomas the animals were not being treated well.

Thomas watched for a while until he became sleepy. He rolled to his back and pulled his hat over his face. He knew that tomorrow would be busy with the burying of their dead and shoring up their defenses. Sleep finally came to him, but just as he entered its realm, he saw the face of the life he had ended.

Once again, his sleep was interrupted. The ground conducted the pounding of horse hooves as they approached

"Thomas Lyle? Thomas Lyle? Where are you?" Thomas stood up and said, "I am Thomas Lyle."

"You are wanted at headquarters by order of General A. P. Hill." The rider turned and rode back into the night.

Thomas was perplexed because he knew it was unusual for a private to meet the commanding general. An order given was an order to be obeyed. He shouldered his rifle and picked up his canteen and haversack. He attempted to brush some of the dirt and dust from his uniform.

He walked along part of the path he had taken earlier to get the ammunition, but this time, he did not have to dodge Federal bullets. He stopped at a water barrel to fill his canteen and wash some of the powder grime from his face.

Not sure exactly where the headquarters tent was be found, Thomas asked for directions. Aided by light from campfires, Thomas walked past rows of the dead laid out for burial. As he passed the hospital tent, he heard a doctor call out for chloroform. He flinched at the reply that there was none left.

A horrified voice shouted, "Don't take off my leg."

A doctor said, "You have no choice. That is the smell of gangrene."

He hurried past as the doctor admonished those attending to hold the unfortunate patient down

The Yankee Present ✷ 29

tightly. An ear-piercing cry rose above the din of the activity of the hospital tent as the doctor began the unpleasant procedure.

As he approached a pile of amputated limbs at the end of an operating table, Thomas was grateful that the surgeon's knife would not have to touch him. He passed a pile of shoes and discarded uniforms. The sights and sounds caused a chill to run along his spine. The smell of death and burnt gunpowder hung heavily in the air.

As Thomas hurried toward headquarters, he passed a group of men having a worship service. In hoarse and haggard voices, they were singing "Rock of Ages." For a moment, Thomas saw the little white church his family attended each Sunday. The third pew on the right side was where the Lyle family sat. Pa, Ma, Samuel, Almeda, Jenny, and he would fill the bench. The Blackwells occupied part of the fourth pew along with the Morgan family.

As he neared the headquarters, he stopped to report to the sentry. Given permission to proceed, he approached the tent. Two officers were sitting under the fly. Thomas halted, squared himself up, and saluted. "Thomas Lyle, Company B of the Tennessee Fourteenth sir."

General Hill stood and said, "Private Lyle, your actions today probably gave us the victory. Your brigade officer has reported that your actions in helping stop the flanking maneuver took General McClelland out of his battle plan. General Jackson and I want to commend you for your actions."

A second officer stepped from under the tent fly and into the light of the lanterns and campfire. Thomas recognized the officer as the rider giving encouragement during the battle. He had heard of the bravery of General Jackson, but he had never seen the general.

"Thank ... thank you, sir," Thomas said.

General Jackson stepped forward and placed patches in Thomas's hand. "Private Lyle, your actions have earned you the rank of sergeant."

Thomas could not believe it. He looked down at the stripes, pulled himself together, and tendered a salute. "Thank you, sir."

"Sergeant Lyle, we need more men of your standing. Wear those stripes proudly," General Jackson said.

"Yes, sir. I'll do my best to honor them," replied Thomas. "Where are you from?" General Jackson asked. "And what about your family?"

"I'm from Lone Oak, Tennessee-at least that is what our family calls it. Some want to call it that because of a large white oak tree near the general store. It's about ten miles south of Clarksville,

Tennessee, where I joined up." Thomas described his family and the farm and was surprised that the general seemed so interested.

"I'm sure you miss your family as I miss mine," General Jackson said sincerely. "I've only seen my baby daughter once since she was born."

General Hill said, "Sergeant Lyle, we need more men like you to win this war. You have been given important responsibility,"

"Yes, sir." Thomas nodded and was dismissed. As he walked back to the front line, he kept looking at the stripes. How would the stripes change his role in the war? He knew the rank would carry new responsibilities. He would be part of the chain of command. Officers above him would depend on his ability to carry out their orders. He would be giving orders, and those he com- manded would have to have confidence in him. He already felt the responsibility.

His thoughts were interrupted by an earnest prayer as he passed the church service. He paused long enough to hear the preacher ask for protection against the heathen Yankee invaders. The prayer ended by requesting safety for each soldier and for the safety of loved ones at home. Resuming his walk, Thomas took a different way to avoid the hospital area.

When he reached the front line, he joined in the frivolity of the day's victory. A round of cheering and congratulations went up from the men as Thomas held up the stripes for everyone to see.

"Good job, Thomas ... uh, Sergeant Lyle, I mean!"

Thomas thanked the men for their comments. "I've got to write my Jenny and tell her about all of this!"

Chapter 4

Thomas located his haversack and sat down by a firepit for light. He found his housewife and unrolled the cloth layer to reveal its contents: needles, thread, and buttons. To the best of his ability, he sewed the stripes to each sleeve. Upon finishing the sewing task, he held up his coat for inspection. His stitches were uneven, and the patch on the left sleeve was not exactly straight. He reasoned his work would be all right for now. Replacing the sewing kit, he pulled the leather roll from the bottom of his haversack. It contained Jenny's letters and his writing paper.

He untied the cord binding the leather. There was one piece of paper left. He had to remember to get some paper the next time a sutler came to camp. As he unrolled the paper sheet from Jenny's letters, he saw Jenny's last letter on top. Thomas removed it from the envelope. He had lost count of the number of times he had read her words, but he wanted to read them one more time. As he began to read, the words seemed to become her voice, bringing them from the wrinkled paper to his ears. Her words had a warming effect on the chilly night air, but they also brought a feeling of homesickness for her and the farm.

My loving Thomas,

I am not sure all my letters have reached you as you have not commented on the news they have contained. I will tell you once again that I am with child. Dr. Ross thinks it will only be a few more weeks before I deliver. It will not be too soon for me

Your mother and I have been making clothes, and Almeda has been knitting a blanket. Samuel has almost finished a crib. He bent some willow pieces to make rockers for its legs. I am so happy that we will have a child for you to come home to. If it is a girl, I would like to name her Olivia in honor of your grandmother. If it is a boy, I want to name him Thomas after you.

Samuel tells me to tell you not to worry about the livestock as he is taking good care of them. He says that when he works with Ada, she does not respond to him as she does to you. Lady mostly lies in front of the porch door to your upstairs room. She does not follow his direction when he tells her to go get Nellie when it is time to do the milking, so he must make the trip to the pasture.

Samuel has moved into our cabin as I have moved into yours and Samuel's room. Your mother said I needed to be closer to her when the baby comes. Samuel had the idea he would sleep and cook for himself there, but after burning most of his meals, he comes to eat Ma's cooking.

Sleeping in your bed does give me feeling of being closer to you. I am so lonely for you. I long for your strong arms to surround me. I miss you whispering my name as we snuggle in bed. I carry your last letter in my apron pocket and find myself reading it several times a day.

Please be careful and safe and come home to me and the baby. I will be totally lost if you don't. I love you so much. All of your family sends their love, and we pray you will be home soon.

Your dearest,

Jenny

Thomas stared at the words until her voice began to fade from his mind. He closed his eyes and saw her running down the road from their cabin as he finished a day's work. She would help him by currying Ada while he put fresh hay and corn in the trough for her to eat. They would walk arm in arm to the cabin porch, climb the steps, and go eat the supper Jenny had prepared.

Afterward, they would spend time on the porch to watch the lightning bugs rise from the hayfield grass. Some nights, Thomas would play his violin. Other nights, they would simply sit in the swing. Jenny would lay her head on Thomas's lap while he smoked his pipe until it was time to go to bed.

He closed his eyes and tried to make his thoughts linger as long as possible.

A wisp of smoke from the campfire filled his nostrils and caused the images to disappear from his mind. Gathering himself, he began to write. It had been a while since he had been able to write, and he had much to tell her.

My dear Jenny,

I love you so much. I miss you so much and long to be home with everyone. I see your face in the clouds. I have dreams of being in your arms. Oh, Jenny, I miss you. I miss you. I pray that this war won't last much longer. I have written once since I received your letter telling me the news of our coming family. It does thrill me, and I cherish the thought of being a father. I long to be back on the farm. I know there is much to do, but I am prepared to stay this course for the cause we are fighting. I know for a fact that I killed a man yesterday in battle. I was first to shoot, and one of the enemies fell. I felt bad for it, but this is war and who knows but what a Yankee bullet might have found its place in me.

Because of something I did in battle, I have been promoted to sergeant. General Hill and General Jackson told me what I did gave us the victory. Our line was being blasted by a couple of cannons. I had been put in charge of a group of men. We were getting low on ammunition, so I went to a supply wagon. Getting back to my group, I had to keep the box hidden so it would not get hit. When I got back to my men, I placed a shot on the Yankee limber box. The gunpowder blew up, knocking the cannons out of use. The Yankees could not flank us, and they soon gave up. The generals gave me sergeant stripes for what I did. I would gladly give up these stripes and walk from Virginia back home *if* this war would end. If I had not joined up so soon, maybe I would have stayed in Tennessee. I would rather be defending my home state, but we are trying to keep the Yankees from getting south. I miss you. I miss the farm and the farmwork I would be doing *if* I were home.

Thank you for the socks you knitted for me. We have marched so much that all of mine had holes in the toes and heels. We often don't have enough tents, so we have to sleep on the bare ground. Please make me blanket of some kind as mine has rips and holes. These mountain nights can get chilly sometimes. I hope I get some new shoes soon as mine are being held together by some rope. I know they won't be new because I will have to take a pair from the pile of shoes that were worn by someone who doesn't need shoes anymore.

I am very tired. It has been a long day. I need to get some sleep because I don't know what we are going to be involved with tomorrow. I love you so very much. Share my news with everyone.

Pray for my safety. I will try to write sooner next time.

Thomas

Chapter 5

"Cook four days of rations and have the company gear loaded and packed on the wagons by daylight tomorrow." It was the first order given by Thomas since being made a sergeant. He had said it as sternly as possible. He knew his orders would need to be sharp, crisp, and given with much resolve so there would be no question about his authority.

He knew what the next four days would have in store for them, but he chose not to reveal exactly what those days would bring. He knew that camp gossip would eventually make its way through the men. To prepare four days of rations would also re- veal their upcoming activity: marching.

The faces standing before him showed fatigue and hunger. Many were barefoot; their calloused feet showed they had been without shoes for quite some time. Tattered coats and pants without knees showed the rugged nature of the fighting they had experienced. They were inadequately equipped, but as Thomas searched their faces, he saw a will and a determination to uphold the cause for which they were assembled. Many, like himself, brought their personal weapons. The uniforms that had been promised had not arrived. Most relied on family to send socks, shirts, or blankets. Spirits were always lifted when a package containing food was received. Cakes or cookies often arrived molded or hard from drying out. Nevertheless, they were enjoyed many times over – even when hardtack was at its best.

Thomas dismissed the men to prepare themselves for completing the order. He, too, had preparations to complete. While his salt pork was frying, he cut a leather string from a piece of harness reins he had found. With the string, he tied the sole of his shoes to what was left of the uppers. His feet also showed the miles of marching. He had walked many miles behind the turning plow Ada pulled. As hard as it was sometimes to walk over the plowed furrows, he wished he were having to keep up with Ada. He hurried to complete his preparations in order to get as much sleep as possible.

Daylight came way too soon, and the day's march began. The objective was to march to Lynchburg, Virginia, and then keep the road open to Richmond so artillery units could freely move.

The march was confined to roads for a while. Cavalry scouts were sent out to reconnoiter the unfamiliar territory. Following the advice of the scouting reports, the column moved from the road to open fields.

Marching across country, to avoid possible Federals and to cover the shortest distance, the army found themselves up to their waists in a swamp. The water and mud were enough of a hindrance, but there were fallen trees hidden under the brackish water.

Swearing at the failure of the cavalry scouts to locate the obstacle became common as feet sank into the mud. The hidden limbs tripped up and scattered the columns. Men stumbled over unseen logs. More than once, Thomas found himself being baptized in the foul-smelling water.

Eventually the water gave way to a mud flat, but a new problem arose.

Someone cried out, "Leeches!"

Thomas found himself joining in the activity of stripping down and scraping leeches from his body.

"Sergeant, you've got 'em on your back," someone yelled. "Let me help you git 'em off."

It took a while, but the last one was finally removed. Thomas was most appreciative for the help.

Columns gradually reformed, and the march began again. The drying clothes soon became drenched from another water source. It began to rain. Rain was not usually enjoyed on a march. However, the rain began to wash away the mud and stench that permeated their clothes. For once, rain was welcomed. A road was finally intersected, and the march gained momentum.

The march continued until dusk. When the rain finally subsided, the sun broke through the clouds. Thomas's clothes were still damp. Fires were quickly built. He scoured the wood- land floor for pine cones and found a broken limb full of pine needles. A soggy pile of pine needles and cones was soon smoldering. He found three sticks and set them up as a tripod. He spread out the wet contents of his haversack as well as his blanket.

Thomas stripped down to his long johns. Soon, his shoes, socks, and clothes were hanging before the sputtering fire. If it wasn't for the pitch-filled pine cones, his fire would have been a poor excuse. Thomas shivered on the soggy blanket and tried to warm himself while drying the only garment he was wearing. The flames wrapped around the sticks he added, and the wet wood hissed. Thomas's thoughts drifted homeward.

The roaring fire in the open fireplace was spreading warmth throughout the room where everyone was gathered. Outside, the ground was covered with shoe top-high snow. Pa was using a piece of windowpane glass to scrape down a piece of seasoned hickory to make a hammer handle. Ma was making a shirt for Samuel, and he was cracking walnuts for a pie Ma had promised to make. Almeda was knitting a blanket to sell to Mrs. Edwards at the general store. Samuel was putting pigs' foot oil on his brogans to make them turn the water and mud from the coming slush of melted snow.

In the corner of the living room stood the decorated cedar Christmas tree. Almeda had tied colored ribbons to the branch tips. Whitewashed sweetgum and sycamore balls also dangled from the branches. Buttons, Almeda's cat, was pawing at a low- hanging sweet gumball. A star was bending over the top growth sprig. The aroma of sassafras tea boiling on the stove came from the kitchen. Thomas was coming through the door with an armload of wood.

Thomas's thoughts were interrupted by the sound of sticks falling beside him. "Hey, Sergeant, we thought you could use some wood for your fire."

Thomas looked up to see Will Harris brushing debris from his bare arm.

"Thank you, Will," Thomas replied as he stood.

For a moment, the two surveyed each other. They both broke into laughter. Thomas was in his long johns, and Will was buck naked.

"We would be up a creek if the Yankees were to attack," Will said.

Thomas chuckled. "You're right about that."

Harris gave a salute, which Thomas returned. They parted laughing at the camp scene. Thomas added wood to the fire and picked up the tripod to rotate a different side to the fire. Thomas looked at his soggy hardtack, and for a moment, he considered eating it. His hand came toward his mouth, but at the last moment, he tossed it into the fire. The side meat was wet, but he put it on the end of a sharp stick and held it over the fire. He hoped the supply wagons would catch up with them soon.

When his clothes were dry, he draped his blanket before the fire and began a check of his command. He wandered about the campfires and made sure his troops were settled.

The cavalry units had reported no Yankees in the area.

Thomas established the order for picket duty. He gathered extra pine needles and tossed them onto his fire. A flash of light and a burst of heat was the result. His blanket now dry, he covered himself. He was glad as an officer he did not have to walk a picket line anymore.

The morning's stillness was interrupted by the shouts of the stevedores as they drove the wagons into camp. Soon, shouts of where certain supplies were to be unloaded brought the camp to life. The wagons were a welcome sight. Food and forage were secured for men and beasts. The warm sunshine and the food lifted the spirits of everyone. At noon, the orders were given to break camp. The march toward Lynchburg resumed.

The outskirts of Lynchburg were reached on the afternoon of the fifth day. Though weary from the march, some set up their tents. Others were too exhausted to make any camp preparations and collapsed.

Their rest was interrupted the next morning when they came under fire from a contingent of invaders. Word passed through the hastily formed lines that they were under fire from McClelland again. Gunboats from the river began a shelling attack.

Orders were to withdraw a safe distance from the river since the army was physically unable to make an effective stand and were not on the ground of their choosing for a battle. Company B was ordered to be a part of the rear guard for the troops as they fell back to better ground. The James River was the divider between the two armies. The Confederates were on the south side, and McClelland was held to the north side.

Numerous skirmishes occurred over the next several days as the road to Richmond was secured. General Lee wanted the road under Confederate control so artillery and supplies could move without concern for the enemy. After securing the road, General Lee formed a unit of men from Georgia, Alabama, and Virginia. More marching ensued as they moved back and forth across northern Virginia, keeping Union troops from Richmond.

Chapter 6

One evening after a day's march Thomas found time to write to Jenny:

Dear Jenny,

I cannot say the words I love you enough. The thoughts of getting this war over and coming home to you keeps me going. I know that I haven't written as often as I should. We have been very busy keeping the Yankees from advancing toward Richmond.

I am fine. Maybe I've lost some weight from all the marching and not having enough to eat at times, but I am all right. If you will make me a shirt and some socks, they would be received with great joy. Tell Ma that a batch of her tea cake cookies would be most welcomed.

I have been in several battles and skirmishes. War is not the glorious thing that some think it should be. I have seen some terrible things. When I am back home on the farm, I hope to be able to forget them. Our scouts learned the Yankees were amassing to push south at a place called Manassas. We did a double-time march to get there first and choose the best field position. There had been a battle there several months ago, and we had a great Southern victory.

What I saw was most terrible. There were blown up wagons, caissons, and cannons. There were rotted remains of horses and mules all over the battlefield. There were bones picked clean by buzzards and wild animals. They were white from the sun.

The worst thing were the skeletons of men, some still covered by their uniforms. It looked like dirt had been put on some of the fallen. However, arms and legs had been uncovered, and the bones were exposed. It made a chill run down my back to think they may have suffered the same fate from the wild animals as the horses. It is very sad to think that no one thought enough to pick up the dead. I know it is not normal to feel sorry for the enemy, but it was a terrible sight.

I don't know when you will get this letter, but it is mid- September here. We have had two battles so far this month. One was at a place called Sharpsburg. We faced a Yank general named Burnside. We pushed him out of the territory.

With no rest, we marched to a town named Shepherdstown. The Yankees had gathered there to cross the Potomac River. Their general must have been crazy. He kept sending formation after formation across the river toward us. None of the enemy ever reached our riverbank. When they finally withdrew, I could have walked across the river on Yankee bodies. The water was red from their blood for hours.

I don't understand how we win so many battles. The Yankees are better equipped, and there are always more of them than us. I guess what matters most is the belief in the cause you are fighting for. It also matters that we are helping the Virginians keep the Yankees from their fields and homes.

When you write again, tell me about how the fall harvesting of crops went. Tell Samuel to keep taking good care of Ada. I hope all of the farmwork is not too much for Pa and Samuel. I pray after each battle this war will end soon. From reports, we hear that thing are not going well in the west.

We have heard that the farts on the Cumberland River have fallen, and that Clarksville is under occupation. I pray that the war does not come to Lone Oak. There is nothing of much importance in the area except maybe the Yankees might forage in the countryside.

Read this letter to the rest of the family. I love you all very much. I promise to take care of myself, but no doubt, we will be in at least a skirmish next week if not sooner. Jenny, tell your folks I think of them also. I must close as orders have been given to cook rations and pack the wagons. This means more marching.

I love you jenny, and I miss you.

*Lovingly,
Thomas*

Chapter 7

Thomas awoke again to the nuzzling of the horse. The muzzle hairs of the horse tickled his cheek and neck. It did not take as long for his eyes to focus in on the horse even though he was looking at the horse upside down. His ears heard an occasional bellow of a bullfrog and the hoot of an owl in the distance. As he regained his senses, he realized his subconscious had replayed the events of the past several months. He shuddered at the thought of remembering the events so clearly.

The lower part of his body was cold, and he realized he was in a creek. Despite the pain and soggy state he was in, he felt comforted by one thought. He no longer heard the rumble of cannon fire or the staccato popping of rifles. Best of all, there were no screams of the dying and no smell of death.

He was breathing cool, clean air- not air filled with stifling smoke from cannons and rifles. His mind, though still somewhat clouded, began to remember the events of the previous day.

They had marched nearly thirty miles in just over two days. Arriving well after sundown, they had not been able to set up much of a camp. Covering the ground with their tents and covering themselves with their blankets, the men had quickly succumbed to their exhaustion.

At dawn, they had formed their lines and prepared for battle. They were still recovering from the miles they had covered from Romney to Winchester by marching the day and most of the night. Underfed and ill-equipped, they dug in behind whatever cover they could find.

The battle started out as light skirmishing, but it escalated into a major confrontation. It was unknown to the Confederates just who the Federal commander was, but it was evident that they were a foe to be reckoned with.

They held their line until noon. When the Federals brought in three additional companies of troops, their part of the line began to fold. The order was given to fall back and reform. He shouted to his men to fall back.

The bushes and brambles were thick, catching his clothes as he ran. The air was full of acrid smoke from the cannon and rifle fire. His eyes were watering, and his lungs were bursting in pain. He stopped running to get his bearings, and he peered through the thick undergrowth, searching for others of his company. Seeing no one, he thought he had not fallen back far enough. He began running again.

A sharp pain ripped through his side and knocked him off his feet. "I'm hit," he said, through clenched teeth. He was confused about who might have shot him. He had definitely been shot from the front, but who was responsible? He thought he had he had been running toward the Southern rear. Surely, he had not been going toward the Federal line.

In anger, he scrambled to his feet and continued to run. He was slowed by the pain. With one hand pressing against his wound, he only had one hand to push aside the branches and briars. His new course took him away from the battle line, and the sound of rifle fire grew faint. He did not know how far he had ran, and he lost all sense of direction. He ran until he felt water splashing around him. He stumbled and tried to regain his balance, but things began to go dark. He slumped to the ground.

Chapter 8

Pa, can Thomas and I go to the Halloween festival at school tonight?" Samuel asked.

Everyone was enjoying Ma's usual Saturday morning breakfast at the table. She had prepared fried side meat, made gravy from the drippings, scramble eggs, fried potatoes, and baked biscuits. There was also butter and milk from the springhouse and blackberry jam made from the berry pickings the previous summer.

As Thomas and Samuel dressed for breakfast, hay had decided Pa would be more inclined to grant their request if Samuel asked since he was younger.

"What's going on?" questioned Pa.

"Oh, the usual: bobbing for apples, s square dancing, and games," Samuel replied as he poured himself another glass of milk.

"Well, besides your usual Saturday chores, I want you to clean out the corn crib. We will start picking corn on Monday. Do any repairs needed, and when you are done, you may go," Pa explained.

"Yes, sir," both boys said at the same time.

Ma admonished the boys to slow down. "I did not raise a couple of pigs," she added.

Saturday chores took less time since Thomas had Samuel's help. Samuel sometimes was able to help a little before he had to leave for school. Besides feeding the livestock for the day, corn had to be shelled for feeding the chickens, and wood had to be chopped for the kitchen stove for the coming week.

After the regular chores, the boys attacked the corn crib. They moved the remaining corn to the front so it would be used first and cleaned up the extra shucks and corncobs. They patched some holes to keep squirrels from getting in for a free meal.

"I wonder how many bushels we will make this year," Samuel said.

"It has been a good year," Thomas said. "The rain came at the right time. No matter how many bushels we make, Old Man Wilson will tell everyone his crop is better than the whole community."

Zeke Wilson was the community's know-it-all. His crops were always better, his mules could pull more, and he always knew the answer to any question. Jumper could tree more squirrels and catch more rabbits than any other dog in the county. His dog was named Jumper because of the way he tracked. Instead of putting his nose to the ground for the scent, he jumped to spot the game he chased since he tracked by sight.

"I wish somebody could put him in his place," Samuel said as they worked. Without much talking, they finished their task. They gathered the tools and returned them to the workshop.

Samuel caught a mischievous grin on Thomas's face as he hung up the last of the tools. "What are you thinking?" Samuel asked.

Thomas gave Samuel a sly wink. "You get the hot water from the kitchen kettle, and I will get the washtub." Samuel re- moved the washtub from the nail on the back porch. "I will meet you upstairs."

They ascended the steps to their room above the porch.

Thomas had a bucket of cold water from the cistern and the kettle of hot water from the stove.

After mixing the water, Thomas turned to Samuel. "Shortest straw wins clean water." Thomas held out the straws for Samuel to pick.

Samuel finally chose the straw in Thomas's left hand. "Dog- gone it." He held up his choice and placed it beside the shorter straw, which Thomas held. "You always win," he said disgustedly.

Years later, Almeda would tell Samuel how Thomas was able to win by using his little finger to break off part of his straw.

Eventually, the boys appeared from their room in clean clothes and their hair combed. Thomas refilled the kettle with water from the cistern, placed it on the stove, and spotted the leftover sausage biscuits from breakfast. They had not stopped to eat dinner as it was more important to finish the crib work.

He took four biscuits and gave two to Samuel as they stepped from the back porch. Lady got up from her spot on the porch and started to follow. Thomas reached down to give her a pat on the head and gently told her to go back and lay down. Lady followed them everywhere as they completed the tasks listed by Pa. She gave a whine, tucked her tail, and stubbornly walked to her spot on the porch.

As they walked past the smokehouse, Thomas ducked in- side. Samuel wondered what Thomas was up to as he disappeared inside, and he was even more perplexed when Thomas emerged with something in a burlap sack.

"What are you doing?" <u>inquired</u> Samuel.

Thomas did not reply, but he motioned for him to follow. They quickly put distance between them and the house, and only when it was out of sight did they slow down.

"What do you have in the bag?" Samuel asked.

"Hog jowl."

"What do we need hog jowl for?" Samuel asked.

Thomas took a moment before he answered. "We will need to keep Jumper busy."

"Keep Jumper busy?" Samuel said. "What are you planning to do?"

"I'm not sure at the moment, but when we get to Zeke's, we can think of something. We'll need the hog jowl to keep Jumper busy-or we will not be able to get into Zeke's yard."

"I thought we were going to the schoolhouse," Samuel stated.

"We are," replied Thomas. "We will go to the school so we can say we went, but we are going to pay Zeke a visit later."

It was almost dark by the time they reached the Lone Oak schoolhouse. Thomas hid the burlap bag under a bush at the corner of the building. They went inside and bought tickets for the various events. Their cousins Harry and Jordan were already there.

Harry spotted Thomas and held up a half-eaten popcorn ball. "You've got to get one of these."

Thomas and Samuel greeted their cousins and asked, "Who all is here?"

They spent most of the next hour playing games, bobbing for apples, and watching the square dancing. Everyone insisted that Thomas play the fiddle. After finishing his tune, Thomas gave Jordan the excuse that he and Samuel had to leave soon.

"Not until you arm wrestle me for a popcorn ball. Loser buys," insisted Jordan.

Thomas gave in to Jordan even though he really wanted to leave. Thomas put up a decent fight so Jordan would think he had actually won. He bought the popcorn ball for a nickel from Mrs. Harris, their teacher. He found Samuel in the crowd, and they got one last apple before slipping out the door.

Thomas retrieved the bag from where it had been hidden.

Samuel asked, "Do you think anyone is suspicious about us leaving early?" Thomas said,

"I don't think so, but I hope no one was minding the time just in case it comes up what time we left."

Samuel and Thomas took advantage of the shadows being cast by an almost full moon as they quickly left school property. "We will go down the Collinsville Road as far as the Morgan property," advised Thomas. "We will use their farm road to get to Zeke's pasture fence line."

The air was cool enough that they could see their breath. At times, the shadows of the partially leafed trees made shadows on the dirt road, which reminded them of ghouls and goblins.

They walked in silence until Samuel asked, "Do you really think Simon Johnson saw a werewolf in these woods?"

Mrs. Harris had read them a story about werewolves and a story about a headless horseman earlier in the week.

Simon had garnered a lot of attention when he claimed he had seen a werewolf on Collinsville Road.

"You can't believe anything Simon says," Thomas said.

Samuel looked behind them. "I guess so, but things sure are spooky tonight."

A brisk walk eventually brought them to the Morgan farm. They found the field road and began the trek toward Zeke's farm. They used the tree-lined pasture fence to bypass the Morgan house and get to Zeke's place.

Getting through the fence, the boys found themselves in Zeke's pasture. Samuel pulled on Thomas's sleeve. "Did you forget about One-Horn Bully?"

Zeke's bull was always ready to fight. One of his horns had been broken off during a fight with the Morgans' bull.

"Yes, I thought about him, but we will just have to keep a sharp eye out for him." Thomas said. "Maybe the darkness will keep us from being noticed."

They made their way across the pasture to the barnyard fence. Most of Zeke's herd was lingering there after the evening feeding. They climbed the plank fence and lowered themselves into the feed lot.

"Be careful where you step," reminded Samuel.

As they made their way across to the yard fence, some of the cows began to move nervously, trying to avoid the intruders.

"So far, so good," whispered Thomas. They paused for a few moments at the yard fence to let the cows settle down. Thomas used the time to find Jumper.

They climbed off the yard fence, and the horrible sound of a rip fell on their ears.

"Oh no," exclaimed Samuel. "I've ripped my coat."

"We will deal with that later," Thomas whispered as he stepped into Zeke's yard. "I'll get Almeda to patch it. She owes me a favor."

As he retrieved the hog jowl from the burlap bag Thomas saw Jumper on the top step of the porch. The restless cows had apparently awakened him. Jumper trotted down the steps and stretched at the bottom. The boys waited nervously to see what he would do next. A light breeze flowing across the yard must have carried a whiff of the meat toward Jumper, and he took a step forward. Jumper's big ears slapped against the side of his neck.

With his right arm, Thomas heaved the jowl like he was playing horseshoes. The meat made an arc across the yard to- ward Jumper's doghouse. The sound of the jowl landing startled Jumper.

Thomas and Samuel waited with anticipation to see what Jumper's response would be. They were relieved that he did not let out one of his long hound dog bays. Instead, Jumper sniffed the air as he followed the trail of scent the jowl made on its trip across the yard. Relief flooded over the boys as Jumper trotted in the direction of the meat offering.

"That should keep him busy for a while," noted Thomas. "What's the next part of the plan?" whispered Samuel. "We could turn over his rain barrel or take the wheels off his buggy," suggested Samuel.

"Let's not mess up his water, and the wheels would take too long," countered Thomas. Just then, he spied Zeke's woodpile. Zeke had four or five ricks of wood cut for the winter. "I've got an idea. Let's stack his wood on the porch in front of his door so he can't get through it in the morning."

"Are you serious?" Samuel asked.

"Yeah," replied Thomas. "We don't want to do anything really bad. We just want to inconvenience him a little and let him know that somebody got close to him."

As they made their way toward the woodpile, Thomas looked back to see what Jumper was doing. The spotted hound's attention was fully on the piece of meat. When they reached the woodpile, they filled their arms with wood. With their arms loaded with as many sticks as they could carry, they crept up to the front porch.

"There is no need for both of us to climb the steps each trip," Thomas said. "You lay your sticks on the end of the porch, and I'll stack them in front of the door."

Samuel began to carry wood to the porch. He laid each stick down individually to avoid making any noise.

The rows began to stack up on the porch. It did not take long to have a shoulder-high stack. By adding crisscrossed sticks to the ends of each row, Thomas was able to increase the height of the rows to the top of the door. The pile of wood was eventually transferred from the yard to the front porch.

From time to time, Thomas looked in the direction of Jumper. Jumper's attention remained fully on the meat. Though the night air was chilly, the boys had sweat on their brows.

Thomas carefully made his way down the porch steps, hoping there would be no creaks to disturb Jumper. Pausing beside one another for a moment to look at the past hour or so of work, the boys realized how tired they were.

As they reached the yard fence, Thomas turned for one last look at Jumper. The full moon cast enough light so that it was almost like day. Jumper was asleep next to what was left of the jowl.

The boys climbed the fence, moved across the barn lot, and jumped over the second fence to the pasture.

"I would give anything to see the look on Zeke's face when he pulls open his door in the morning. All he will see are the ends of the sticks," Thomas said with a chuckle.

Samuel produced a slight grin.

They made their way back to their farm, crossed the creek, and made their way up the hill past the horse stable and corn crib to the smokehouse. When they reached the corner of the smokehouse, Thomas stopped suddenly. "Oh no. I left the burlap bag."

Samuel said, "maybe Zeke will think it is one that he dropped." "I doubt it when he smells the meat," Thomas said.

As they made their way across the yard, Lady trotted over to meet them.

Thomas reached out to give her a pat on the head. Lady began to lick his hands.

"She can still smell the meat on my hands," Thomas said.

"Remind me to wash my hands really well in the morning so no one will know I handled the hog jowl."

They reached the porch and sat down on the rock step to take off their shoes.

"Walk next to the sides of the steps," Thomas said. "Why?" Samuel asked.

"The steps will be less likely to creak next to the wall," Thomas said.

The boys cautiously made their way up their room. They felt their way around the dark room to find their beds. As tired as they were, it did not take long for sleep to settle over them.

So soundly were the boys asleep that they did not hear Pa open the door at the bottom of their steps. However, when Pa re- ported that it was the second time he had called-and there was a special emphasis on second time, - Thomas and Samuel were up immediately.

Quickly dressing and washing up, the boys slid silently into their seats at the table.

"You boys must have gotten in late last night," Pa said sternly.

"I'm not sure what time it was," said Thomas. "Did you have fun?" Almeda asked. "Enough," said Pa.

Ma said, "The food has been blessed. Eat-and get your morning chores done. We will not be late for church."

"Yes, ma'am," Thomas and Samuel answered together. For a while, everyone was busy eating.

Pa finally said, "Ma, when I went out to the smokehouse to get the jowl for you, I counted six. I thought we had seven."

Ma looked up in surprise. "Yes, we had seven. What happened to the other one?"

"Maybe we did miscount." Pa did not seem completely satisfied with his statement. The boys were very interested in their plates of food.

On Monday evening, Ma called them for suppertime. Everyone filled their respective seats, and the meal began after Pa offered the blessing.

After a while, Pa said, "I ran into Zeke Wilson at the store. He was telling some story about a prank someone pulled on him on Saturday night. Of course, it was a Halloween prank someone had done on him. He said he found a burlap bag that was not his in his yard, and it appeared that Jumper had had a nice meal of a hog jowl. The thing he laughed the most about was that someone had stacked his woodpile on his front porch in front of his door. I guess someone thought he would be inconvenienced and not be able to get out his door. Zeke said he would just have to go in and out the back door until he used enough wood to get his front door open. The thing Zeke was most appreciative about was that someone had stacked his winter wood on the porch out of the rain and snow."

Thomas and Samuel knew better than to look at each other as they busied themselves with the food on their plates.

Samuel asked Almeda to pass the butter as he reached for another biscuit. She hid a smile as she wiped her mouth with her apron.

Chapter 9

Thomas was brought to his senses again by a nudge from the horse. The horse was impatiently pawing the ground. The big animal lowered its head, and its bridle reins fell within reach of Thomas. He took hold of them and rolled over to his hands and knees. His canteen and haversack were close by. He secured them in his grip. He looked for his rifle, but he did not see it in the darkness. He decided that he probably lost it when he was shot, but he decided not to worry about losing his weapon.

He summoned every bit of energy from within and struggled to stand up. Though his vision was still somewhat cloudy, the moonlight was so bright that Thomas could see the horse was a big roan. He swept his hand along the horse's neck down to the shoulder and was surprised to find the horse was still saddled. He gathered all his strength, got his foot in the stirrup, and pulled himself up into the saddle. Pain ripped through his side, and an utterance slipped between his tightly clenched teeth.

The horse immediately turned and started walking. Thomas did not know where he was going, but he really didn't care. He knew that a saddled horse must have a stable somewhere.

He did not know how far he rode. He eventually came to a house, and the horse stopped at the gate. In the moonlight, Thomas saw a two-room log cabin with a dogtrot between. He could see a dim light coming from a window. He slid from the saddle, moved through the gate, and stumbled up a short path.

A large rock slab made a step up to the porch. He reached for a porch column to steady himself. He put one foot on the step, pulled his shaky figure up on the plank floor, and walked slowly toward the door.

He knocked and waited. He felt his strength waning because of the exertion it had taken to get from the horse to the door. Things were going dark, and he felt his knees starting to buckle as the door opened. He fell into outstretched arms.

The soft glow of a lamp illuminated the kitchen. A woman helped him to a cot. She placed a pillow under his head and pulled a chair closer. Even in the dim light, he could tell she was quite beautiful.

She pulled off his brogans and placed a shawl over him. "There ... just lie back and let me look at you." Her voice was gentle and reassuring as she adjusted the cover. She pulled the lamp closer, unbuttoned his coat, and taking scissors from her apron she cut open his shirt.

She frowned as she inspected the wound. She washed away the blood with water from a kettle. She moved across the room, and he heard the rattle of utensils in a drawer.

She placed a knife in the coals of the firebox of the stove. She took a crock jug down from a shelf and said, "Whiskey ... take a sip." She put the jug to his lips.

The whiskey burned all the way down to his stomach. He had never tasted whiskey or felt its burn. He managed to sup- press a cough for a moment, but when he inhaled, the vapors filled his lungs. A cough eventually escaped from his throat.

He hoped it would not take much to deaden the pain when the bullet was removed.

She poured some whiskey on the wound, and it felt like a fireball rolling over his body. She put the jug to his lips and said, "Take some more."

The second drink was not as breathtaking. A third and fourth sip were taken.

After a few minutes, the room began to go blurry.

"Place this spoon handle between your teeth," she said. She moved the lamp closer and retrieved the knife from the firebox.

Thomas saw the glowing, red-hot tip of the blade as she brought it closer. The whiskey had not deadened his senses enough. He heard the sizzle of his flesh burning and saw a wisp of smoke rising and felt the knife probing his side. He bit down so hard on the spoon handle that it cracked. She turned her head to avoid the wisp of smoke.

The intense pain was lessened when his eyes met hers.

"I've got to get it." She dropped the minie ball onto the table and poured more whiskey into the wound. He arched his back and winced in pain.

She cleaned the wound with more warm water. He heard the ripping of cloth, and he felt the fold of a bandage laid on the wound.

Their eyes met once more, and the last thing Thomas saw was her face as the room began to grow dark.

Chapter 10

On Saturday afternoon, Thomas sat on the front porch and waited for the rest of the family. He had come in from the hay-field early to clean up for the corn shucking at the Blackwell farm. He and Pa had been trying to get up one last batch of fall hay. They had left some of the hay on the wagon for the hayride to the Blackwell farm.

Thomas waited impatiently for the rest of the family. His mother was finishing a pot of her famous chicken and dump-lings in the kitchen. Other ladies of the community would have their special dishes. He had heard that Mr. Blackwell had barbe-cued a hog. There would be a lot of food, but that was not the only reason Thomas wanted to get going soon.

Thomas's team had been beaten at the last corn shucking. A little move by one of the Johnson boys had cost them the chance to win. He wanted to show the Johnsons who the best team was. He was counting on his cousins Harry, William, and Jordan to be there. Samuel would be the fifth team member.

Thomas's thoughts were interrupted by Lady pushing her nose under his armpit. He turned in her direction to see a pair of brown eyes staring at him. "What do you want?" he asked needlessly.

Giving Lady the desired attention she longed for, Thomas resumed his thoughts of the upcoming trip to the Blackwell farm as he began to scratch behind the upturned ears.

Mr. Blackwell would already have his corn in a large pile. If his corn yield had been as good as the Lyle farm, there would be a large pile. It had been a good season. Thomas wanted to get the team together to talk about things before the Johnson boys arrived.

Harry would be the runner. He was not the fastest, but he was very strong. The shuckers would fill the basket. If the basket was not full enough, Mr. Blackwell could send them back to the pile of corn ears. This kept a team from carrying only partially filled baskets to have a higher number of baskets. The team with the most baskets shucked would be the winner. They would have to shuck like they had never shucked before to beat the Johnsons. There was still some talk about Harry getting tripped, which caused him to fall at the shucking at the Miller farm.

Orville Johnson had stuck out his foot, causing Harry to land in a heap along with his basket of corn. Besides the bragging rights of being the first-place team, the winning team got to get their food first. Being first in line did not matter to Thomas as much as putting the Johnsons in their place.

The rest of the family appeared on the front porch, and family and food were soon loaded on the wagon. The fresh hay softened the road bumps as they made their way toward the Blackwell farm. As they rode along, Thomas thought about himself and his family.

Thomas was usually described as being tall and lanky. His hair and eyes were the same color as his brown felt farm hat. From brow to the bottom of his chin produced a rather long face. However, his long face was proportional to his height, and the ruddy complexion provided quite a handsome appearance. He always scoffed at Almeda's remarks about the young ladies of the community taking notice of his features. Thomas usually had his mind on other matters, and he was unaware of their subtle glances.

Samuel was the youngest of the three Lyle children. His appearance was quite the opposite of Thomas. He was short and stocky with very light hair. Even though he was four years younger, his muscular frame allowed him to keep up with Thomas as they did the farmwork. Samuel idolized his older brother, and the two boys had a very special bond.

Almeda was very much like Ma. Her chestnut brown hair was usually parted to produce two long braids that fell off her shoulders. She was very domestic with her sewing and crocheting. She and Ma often joined the other ladies of the community in quilting and sewing. Grandmother Olivia had taught her how to tat, and she had produced beautiful lace for collars and sleeve cuffs. She was becoming an experienced cook, and she helped with the summer food preservation. Anyone treating her unjustly could expect to hear from Thomas and Samuel.

John Lyle was a man of impeccable character. He was of medium build, and his sunburnt face and numerous wrinkles reflected his work ethic. Fair in his dealings with others, his word was his bond. He had been known to walk the two miles back to Lone General Store to return too much change from a purchase.

He'd been hurt when a tree lap he was cutting on rolled unexpectedly on his leg. Although the leg was not broken, it was injured enough to leave him with an unmistakable limp.

Margaret Lyle was a woman with much love, but anyone who tried her patience knew she had another side as well. As a mother hen takes care of her brood, Ma was loving but also firm in her direction. Her graying black hair and slightly bent frame were an indication that farm life had been challenging for her.

Her days were spent cooking, washing, ironing, and doing chores. She was also the family doctor. Besides the cuts, scratches, and bruises of the family, she also doctored the animals when needed. She had assisted in the birthing of many of the farm animals. All this activity kept her days full. Love abounded within her for those she cared for, and in return, she was the recipient of much love from her family and those who knew her.

"Whoa," Pa said as he pulled on the reins of the team of horses. They had arrived at the Blackwells.

Thomas dangled his leg over the side of the wagon. Before sliding to the ground, he looked around at the crowd. It looked like the whole community of Lone Oak was already there.

While the horses were being hitched to a tree, Thomas took his mother's pot of dumplings to the food tables. The aroma of frying chicken, cooking stews and vegetables, and pies and cakes filled the air. The hog on the spit was making everyone's mouth water.

Setting the dumplings down, Thomas turned to look for his cousins. Seeing them by the well, Thomas waved and started to- ward them. As he passed a group of men, he heard Zeke Wilson bragging about his corn crop. "I'm going to have to board up one of my barn stalls because my corn crib won't hold my crop," he said.

Always bragging about something, Thomas thought.

The Johnsons were standing off to one side with sly grins across their faces. Their looks only fueled Thomas's desire to win.

While Mr. Blackwell finished with the barbecue, Thomas got the team together for a pep talk.

"Just look at the Johnsons," said Harry.

"Yeah, just look how confident they are," quipped William. "We have to give all we've got," added Thomas.

Mr. Blackwell had made a large pile of corn near his crib. The pile was fifty or so paces from the corn crib. A stack of baskets was nearby. The teams would fill the baskets with as much as a person could carry. The object was to shuck the most baskets of corn. With no shucks on the ears of corn, the corn weevils would have no place to hide.

Mr. Blackwell would keep count of the number of baskets each team brought to the crib. Besides the Lyle and Johnson teams, there were two other teams. The Abernathy boys lived on the farm south of the Blackwells, and the Morgan cousins would be their competition.

Mr. Blackwell made his way to the crib and slid back the latch holding the door shut.

Thomas and his team stood in anticipation of the event. The Johnsons had been trying to upset Thomas. "Don't listen to them," Thomas said. "They just want to get us flustered so we will not work together."

Mr. Blackwell climbed the step to stand in the doorway to take the baskets of corn. After emptying each basket, he would drop the basket to the ground for the runner to carry it back to those shucking on the next basket. "It's good to see everybody," he began. "There is plenty of food, and we are here to have some fun and games. It's always good for our community to get together for things like this. We had a good summer, and we have been blessed with a good harvest.

"After the shucking, we will eat and enjoy the games. We have a place for horseshoes. I've cleared a spot for marbles, and I know that you ladies think the tobacco spitting is... well, the men know what you think. When it gets dark, I'll light the bonfire. I know somebody will get out a banjo and a fiddle. Let's have a good time and enjoy our time together.

"Are the shucking teams ready? Let me go over the rules. One team member will be the runner for the entire event. The other four will be the shuckers. The runner must set the basket of corn up here on the door threshold. There will be no interference from one team member toward another team member. Remember the red ear rule. Anyone shucking a red ear must kiss the closest unmarried female. I don't know why, but even in my field of white corn, a red ear will appear sometimes. Teams ready?" Mr. Blackwell looked at each of the teams. "Then go!"

The teams jumped to the pile, and shucks began to fill the air. The younger ladies and girls gathered the shucks to keep the area clean. The shucks would be used to fill mattresses and pillows. Some corn shuck dolls might be made for the young girls. Most of the shucks would end up feeding livestock.

Encouraging shouts filled the air as the onlookers pulled for their teams. The shucking and the girls scurrying about became the center of activity. Tally marks began to go down beside the team names.

As soon as the four shuckers filled a basket, Harry would grab it and run for the corn crib. Thomas and the others would almost have the next basket full by the time Harry returned. Thomas made sure each basket had enough ears to corn so that Harry would not have to make more trips than necessary, but the basket must not weigh so much that Harry would struggle to carry it. One extra trip could be the difference between winning and losing.

The pile of corn began to disappear. Their team was definitely ahead of the Abernathys, and the Abernathys were ahead of the Morgans. Thomas was not worried about them. It was the Johnsons he wanted to beat. "Remember last time," he said as Harry grabbed a basket and started for the crib.

As Thomas looked over at the Johnsons, everyone began to laugh and shout. It took him a moment to realize they were staring at him. *What is wrong?* He looked down and saw what he was holding. *A red ear of corn? Oh no, not a red ear.* He realized he was wasting precious time.

He threw the ear into their basket and turned to find the closest girl. He ran to the nearest girl, spun her around, and planted a kiss on her cheek. The crowd cheered, and as Thomas stepped back, he realized he had kissed Jenny Blackwell.

Jenny giggled and ran to a group of her friends.

Thomas felt his ears grow hot with embarrassment. He was frozen in his tracks.

Harry shouted, "Come on, Thomas." He had an empty basket. Thomas quickly made his way back to the team.

"This will be basket number twenty-seven for us, and the Johnsons have twenty-six," reported William.

Orville Johnson started to the crib with basket number twenty-seven.

Jordan said, "We are tied now."

The shucking grew more furious for the next few minutes until there were only a few ears left. The Abernathy and Morgan teams dropped out, and the battle was between the Lyles and the Johnsons.

Orville managed to rake together a few ears for their last basket. That left too many ears for Harry to carry in one basket. If they left ears which that be picked up by the Johnson team, Orville and his brothers would win.

"Put 'em all in this basket," Harry said. "It will be too heavy," Jordan replied. "No, I can do it," Harry said.

They finished last ears and shoved them into the basket.

Harry picked up the basket and staggered toward the corn crib.

When Harry was halfway to the crib, Asa Johnson caught up with him.

"Watch out for Asa," Thomas yelled.

Asa moved closer, and Harry stopped in his tracks. With noting to bump into, Asa lost his balance and fell, spilling the corn from his basket. Harry continued toward Mr. Blackwell, staggering under the weight of his overly filled basket.

Asa refilled his basket and started for the crib. Harry reached the crib door a few steps before Asa.

A cheer rose from the crowd, but Thomas and his team celebrated the loudest.

Harry, Jordan, William, Samuel, and Thomas found themselves in a pile at the crib door. They had won: 37- 36.

Thomas and his cousins slapped each other on the back and hugged.

Jordan did a backflip that brought cheers from the crowd. They eventually settled down and started for the food tables. The other teams joined them, and they all began to fill their plates. The Johnsons, being mad they had lost, boarded their wagon. Orville brought the reins down hard on the backs of his team of mules as they left. Angry shouts could be heard for some time as he admonished the hapless animals to go faster.

With the competition over and friendships returned, everyone was ready to enjoy the rest of the evening. A fiddle and a banjo appeared, and it was not long before music filled the air.

Mr. Blackwell tossed his hat into the air as he began to buck dance. The clanging of horseshoes resounded from the horse- shoe stakes. The younger boys were down on their knees shooting marbles. The older boys were playing mumblety-peg. Jugs of apple cider, which had been cooling in the cistern, were pulled up and carried to the food tables. With full plates and cups, the eating and fun continued.

Thomas lost count of the times he visited the wagons to refill his plate. He kept his eye on his aunt Nell's black walnut pie plate. Just before the last piece was taken, he took the pie plate, so he could get all the tidbits left from the other pieces of pie as well as the last piece.

Mrs. Blackwell began to organize lines for the Virginia reel and encouraged Thomas to join. It wasn't that Thomas was too tired to dance, but he was still embarrassed that he had kissed Jenny. If he was lucky, he might not have to dance with her. He failed to realize that Mrs. Blackwell was counting places in the line of men to know where Jenny should line up.

It eventually happened. Thomas found himself bowing to Jenny. She curtsied, and they promenaded to the end of the line and back to their starting places.

Thomas glanced at Jenny. "Don't be embarrassed," she said.

As other couples took their turns, he found himself thinking about how different it was dancing with Jenny. It was somehow different from the other girls he had danced with.

Jenny glanced in the direction of her mother, and Mrs. Blackwell nodded.

The frivolity continued with square dancing and clogging, which fueled everyone's appetites. The clang of a horseshoe game occasionally brought a shout. Some of the men had a tobacco spitting contest. Fiddle and banjo music filled the air. Thomas suddenly found a fiddle thrust into his hands. With much coaxing, he finally played his favorite song.

Mr. Blackwell lit the pile of wood for the bonfire. As the flames rose higher and higher, they illuminated the backyard and the crib wall. Dancing couples cast shadows on the graying planks. Some did funny things to their shadows, which brought merriment to the party.

Gradually, the sounds of music and stomping feet subsided. The last kettle was scraped, and the fire was doused.

As Thomas and his team were saying goodbye, Mr. Blackwell approached. "Thanks for helping me get my corn into the crib. I have something here for the winning team, but don't let the others know about it." He slipped a silver dollar into each boy's hand.

For a moment, they could only look at the shiny coin. "Thank you "

Everything and everyone loaded onto their wagon, the Lyles eventually made their way home. An enjoyable time had been had by all, especially for Thomas. Tired as he was, he still relished the victory.

Thomas lay back on the soft hay with his hands under his head and looked up into the night sky. Oh, what was the glory in winning a corn shucking? Not much in the scheme of life, but Thomas and his cousins always enjoyed the activities they participated in.

He was brought back to the present by a jolt from the wagon as a wheel found a rut in the road. He had noticed his father in conversation with other men of the community. From the grim looks on their faces, the subject appeared to be serious.

"Pa, what were you and the other men talking about?" "Political things."

Ma said, "Political things? John, why must you men always talk about political things?"

"I am afraid war is coming," Pa said sadly. "Uncle Solomon Dudley showed us an article from the Clarksville paper. More states have seceded from the Union. There is growing sentiment from some Tennesseans for Governor Harris to call for a secession vote. President Lincoln has called for seventy-five thousand volunteers to put down what the North is calling a rebellion. Like I have always said, we don't now or will we ever own a man. If you boys and me can't get the work done, it just won't get done."

After a somber pause, Pa said, "The North has had slaves for years, and now they want to tell the South that it is wrong to have slaves? They will not pay a decent price for our crops, yet they put taxes on what we sell to Europe. If Lincoln isn't planning for war, why does he need all these additional troops? Grandfather Fletcher says he truly believes the North is going to invade the South soon."

Samuel said, "Pa, what is going to happen?"

"If Tennessee secedes, then we will be expected to supply troops," Pa answered. "I can't fight because of my legs, and you are too young, but Thomas may have to go."

Hearing these words brought Thomas to an upright position. He stared at his father.

His mother gasped. "John, don't say such things." She put her shawl to her mouth. "No, no, no ... not my boys."

They rode the rest of the way in silence. The only sounds were the plodding of the horse's hooves on the dusty road and the jingle of the trace chains from the harness.

War? Thomas could not imagine what war must be like. He knew that it must be terrible to have to shoot at another person. *What is it like to be shot?*

In Clarksville, Thomas had heard people bragging about how the South would whip the north, but he had not recognized the serious nature of the remarks.

Because it was very late by the time the family reached home, Pa drove past the stables and on up the hill to their house. The hay was taken from the wagon for the horses which were tied to the hitching post in the back yard. The harness was removed and placed on the wagon. Things would be ready for church the next day.

Thomas and Samuel climbed the stairs to their room. Thomas was still in a daze from Pa's remarks. He simply laid down on his bed without undressing. He did not understand all about the political things of which Pa had discussed. He knew enough however that if the North invaded the South, then the South would surely defend itself. To defend themselves, the South would need an army- an army of which he might be a part.

Samuel blew out the lamp, and Thomas closed his eyes. For a brief moment, he saw Jenny's face. Why had he seen her image? *Tomorrow is Sunday, and I will see jenny at church. Will she avoid him because of the kiss? I hope Harry and the others do not kid me.* He realized he was beginning to have feelings for her he could not explain.

Chapter 11

When Thomas awoke the next morning, his nostrils were full of the smell of baking biscuits and frying meat. He opened his eyes and saw her standing by the stove. Her golden hair rippled down her back. Around her waist was a white apron, and her dress was the same blue gingham square material as the window curtains. Her moccasin-covered feet made no noise as she moved.

She moved lightly across the floor as if she were floating. She turned to bring a platter to the table. Her eyes met his, and she smiled. "Good morning." She set the platter on the table, pulled a bench from under the table, and sat down next to him. "My name is Abigail McAllister."

"I am Thomas Hanner Lyle from Montgomery County, Tennessee. I got separated from my unit yesterday- at least I think it was yesterday. We were in a battle at a place called Shepherdstown."

"Shepherdstown is about five miles from here. I heard cannon fire all day yesterday. Twice, Yankee soldiers rode by here headed in that direction two days ago. I hid so they would think the place was deserted. I put Jake and the cow in the barn, so they would not be seen. Do you remember Big Jake bringing you here last night?"

She further explained about her visit to the neighbors yesterday. When she returned home, she brought in a sack of vegetables before putting Jake in the barn lot. By the time she had stopped to put Jake up, he had wandered off. "I wasn't worried because he has done that before, and he always comes back."

Thomas felt his side. It hurt but not as much as yesterday. "After we eat, I'll dress your wound again," Abigail said.

They had a breakfast of biscuits, side meat, peach preserves, and fresh milk.

As she moved to clear the table, Thomas watched her every move. In many ways, she reminded him of Jenny. They both had long, golden hair. They were about the same height and had slender waists.

She began to sing, and then she stopped abruptly.

"Don't stop," Thomas implored. He could tell it was a church hymn, but he did not know the words.

Her voice was soft and clear like Jenny's.

When she finished with the dishes, she got the whiskey jug and cut some cloth strips. Her fingers moved tenderly as she replaced the bandage. The whiskey-soaked cloth did not burn a much as the night before. Thomas watched her face, and their eyes met occasionally.

"You are lucky. The ball did not go too deep. Your coat probably helped stop the lead ball."

"We were ordered to fall back and regroup," he said. "I thought I was going to the rear of our line, but I may have lost my bearing due to all of the smoke from the rifles and cannons. The woods were full of men shouting and the cries of the wounded. I guess I just got lost. I don1t think I would have been shot by one of my own men, but I just don1t know." Thomas buried his head in his hands.

Abigail took his hands in hers. "I am sure war can be very confusing. The shouting, the loud noises, the cries of the wounded, and I can1t imagine what else." She finished with the new bandage.

Thomas saw the broken spoon on the table. "I'm sorry about the spoon." He picked it up and examined it.

"Oh, don't worry," Abigail said. "Caleb will whittle another for me when he comes home." She went to the other room and brought back some of Caleb's clothes. "Change into to these while I check on the fire."

Thomas heard the splash of water being added to the wash kettle. He changed into Caleb's clothes as quickly as possible.

Abigail gathered his clothes and put them in the kettle.

It was noted Caleb's shirt sleeves and pants legs were a little short for Thomas.

He rested for the remainder of the day, and Abigail did her chores. After his clothes dried, she got her sewing basket and mended his coat. She said, "The stripes on your sleeves are a little crooked."

"I was excited about getting them and was exhausted from the day's battle when I sewed them on."

Abigail cut his crude stitches to remove the insignias. She carefully positioned the stripes on his jacket and reattached them with even stitches.

"There now." She held up the jacket up for Thomas to see.

"Thank you. It's easy to see that I cannot sew," he said. Abigail had also stitched up the bullet hole.

Abigail spent the afternoon preparing vegetables for drying. She cut potatoes and squash in thin slices and put them out in the sun to dry. She chopped up cabbage to start a crock of kraut. In another crock jar, she started pickles.

Late in the afternoon, she took the milk pail and went to the barn to milk the cow. When she returned, she prepared the evening meal.

They ate fresh vegetables and drank the warm milk. It had been a long time since Thomas had enjoyed fresh vegetables. For months, most of his meals had been little more than hardtack, salt pork, or beef and parched corn coffee.

Night eventually fell. The light from the fireplace cast a glow across the floor.

"How did you get the stripes on your jacket?" Abigail asked as she added wood to the fire.

Thomas related the events of the battle. "I don't think of myself as doing anything heroic. I was just being a soldier."

"My husband joined the Twenty-Eighth Virginia," she said. "The last letter I had from him; he was in someplace called Manassas. The Yankees were gathering there, and a battle was sure to happen. That was several months ago, and I have not heard from him since. I pray that he is safe. With all the marching from place to place, maybe he has not had the time to write-or maybe his letters just got lost."

They talked for a while trading family information. Caleb and Abigail had gone to the same school. Caleb's father operated the local general store. When Abigail's parents would come to buy supplies, Caleb would sneak Abigail candy from the candy Jar.

In time, Abigail's attraction toward Caleb was more than filling her sweet tooth. "Besides being handsome, he was kind and gentle. I wanted him to ask me to marry, but I was afraid he might not ask because my parents were not as rich as his."

For a moment Thomas was silent. "I don't think that probably ever entered his mind," he said as he surveyed her features.

Eventually Caleb asked her to marry him, and they had turned the little homestead into a nice little farm. Caleb had been gone almost two years. During that time, Abigail had cared for the farm. The planting, cultivating, and the harvesting had all been done with little help from neighbors.

"My neighbor, Noah Wallace, comes over to do the spring plowing. I planted the corn patch on the other side of the barn. I put out my garden, but I had to wait for him to get his spring crops out first. That is why my garden vegetables are not ready for picking," she explained. "I surely hope that we do not have an early frost. If we do, I will lose many of my vegetables."

Thomas said, "I grew up in the house my great-grandfather built. It is on a hill overlooking a lot of our farm. The oak and maple trees give us a lot of shade. A creek runs through the farm, and Samuel, my younger brother, and I go fishing and swimming there. I have a younger sister named Almeda." Thomas told her about the cabin where he and Jenny lived.

The ray of moonlight coming through the window that had started on one side of the room had moved to the other side of the room by the time they finished talking.

Abigail got up and moved to the door.

Thomas settled back on the cot as she stepped down to the dogtrot and closed the door. He heard the door to the room across the dogtrot open and close. He pulled the quilt closer to his chin and closed his eyes.

He said a prayer for his family at home, especially for Jenny. He also lifted up Abigail. He thought about her not hearing from Caleb for so long. He thought about the Manassas battlefield he had seen. Could Caleb still be there? He chose to think she was right. Maybe he had just been too busy to write. After all, he knew how much marching he had been through for the past several months. He decided not to tell Abigail about the things he had seen at Manassas.

Chapter 12

Thomas was awakened the second morning by the crowing of a rooster. He raised up on one elbow and looked around the room. Then, with a little effort, he swung his legs over the side of the cot and sat up. The twisting did not produce much pain in his side. His head was much clearer than the day before.

He surveyed the room and saw strings of dried vegetables hanging from pegs on the log walls. There were strings of potato, pumpkin, and squash. There was a cabinet of shelves with a curtain hanging on a string. One side of the curtain was partially open, and he could see pewter plates and cups on the shelves. Pots and utensils were hanging on pegs.

Besides the cookstove was a large fireplace made from large fieldstones. Bunches of onions and garlic hung from the rafters. Several varieties of herbs were drying beside the fireplace. Wild sage was the only one he recognized. There were tied bunches of other plants with small brown pods attached to their roots. Thomas would later learn these plants were called peanuts, and he would learn they were quite tasty.

There was a violin and bow resting on the mantel above the fireplace between two lamps. A table with two benches occupied the center of the room. Besides the cot, there were two straight-backed chairs and a rocking chair. A shotgun rested on pegs over the back door. A fringed leather haversack hung nearby, and Thomas assumed it held patches and ammunition.

The morning's stillness was shattered by the sound of someone chopping wood. Thomas stood up slowly and walked to the back door. He saw Abigail at the woodpile.

She was wielding an ax as well as any man. She lifted it high above her head before bringing it down upon the blocks of wood she was splitting. She split some of the blocks with one blow. It was amazing to Thomas that she could be so strong in this chore while being so tender and delicate when she dressed his wound.

She picked up an armful of her labor and turned to walk to the cabin.

Thomas said, "Good morning." "Good morning."

Thomas replied, "I feel almost good enough to help."

"I can manage," she said. "Don't do anything to open your wound."

He stepped aside so she could enter the cabin. She dropped the wood in the woodbox and turned around. She had already been to the spring to get a pail of water. She offered Thomas a mug, and it was the coolest, sweetest water he had tasted since he left the farm back in Tennessee.

As he finished the last swallow, drops ran down his chin. As Thomas wiped his chin, a slight burp escaped. Embarrassed, he offered an apology for his ill manners. A feeling of weakness began to overcome him, and he shuffled to the bench.

"Don't overdo it," Abigail said. "It will take a few days to get your strength back. After breakfast, I will change the bandages and get you out in the yard hammock in the sun. It will help build up your strength."

When they had finished breakfast and replaced the bandages, Abigail led Thomas to the hammock, which was attached to two oak trees. She slipped a pillow under his head and smiled. "There. Just relax and take in the morning sun."

The sun covered his body like a blanket. Drowsiness flooded over Thomas, and he fell asleep. He began to dream about plowing on the farm back home.

"Whoa, Ada," Thomas said as the big Belgian horse reached the end of the row. Thomas turned and surveyed the long row of freshly turned earth. It glistened in the sunlight, and birds were already searching for worms among the clods of rich soil. Thomas paused for a moment to watch them flutter from clod to clod as the birds pulled their finds from the soil. He watched with amusement as two birds fixed on the same worm, and a brief scuffle of flapping wings and chirps ensued.

He could almost see the row of corn that would grow there. After plowing, he would harrow the ridges down as level as possible. He would go to the Blackwells and borrow the corn planter that Pa and Mr. Blackwell had bought together last year. Pa was shelling corn from last year's crop to be planted.

"Time for a breather, old girl?" he asked. "If not for you, at least for me." Thomas tied the reins to the plow handle, patted the rump of the big beast, and walked over to the tree branch where he had hung his water keg. Lady had followed him to the field and got up to greet him with a wag of her tail. She followed Thomas everywhere he went. She would watch whatever task Thomas was involved in. She could watch him work for hours. Thomas reached down and gave her the attention she craved, a pat on the head and a scratch behind an ear.

The water had warmed in the heat. He decided to give Ada a break from plowing. He emptied the keg into his hat for her to drink and patted the thick, stout, brown neck on the seventeen- hands-high body. The light-yellow mane was trimmed evenly, and there were yellow stockings above the big hooves. Ada was so strong that she could pull the single pointed turning plow by herself.

It would be a short walk to the beech tree spring. The spring had been a source of water for the family since Thomas's grandfather had cut the limestone to wall it up. The spring's runoff flowed to Hurricane Creek, which had been named by his great grandfather. The creek was fed by many springs as it made its way through the Lyle farm. When working in any of their fields, they were never far from a spring that provided refreshing water.

Thomas reached the spring by the path through the woods and knelt down to fill his keg. He pulled the plug from the spout and pushed it under the water. The bubbles burst from the small opening as water filled the wooden container. As the keg filled, the bubbles escaped faster and pitch became higher.

When the last bubble broke the water surface, Thomas replaced the plug in the spout. Setting the keg aside, he lay down to bring his face close to the cool water. After drinking his fill of the clear water, he closed his eyes and lowered his head. The cool water quickly took the heat from his face.

He stood up quickly and let the water drain onto his shirt. Thomas stripped several leaves from the peppermint plants that grew around the spring. The mint and water were very refreshing. As he sat on the rock wall, he observed the spring keepers skimming over the water surface. Lady had submerged herself in the water also and gave an occasional snap at a passing dragonfly.

He could only guess how old the beech tree was. There was a date- 1792 - carved into the tree. It was generally thought that great-grandfather Augustus had put the date on the tree as a young boy when his family had come from Pittsylvania County, Virginia. Thomas's great-grandfather had been given a block of acres for his role in the Revolutionary War. Much of the land had been sold or given to other family members. The Lyle family farm had two hundred acres of some of the best since it had plenty of fresh water.

Thomas had spent the better part of an afternoon carving his initials into the smooth bark almost two years before. He reached up to touch the scar forming as the ageless tree healed itself. He ran his finger along each letter. He visualized the tree standing as a sentinel over the spring long after he found his resting place under the cedars of the family cemetery on the hill across the way. He remembered the blister the knife had produced.

The short rest came to an end, and he began the trip up the path. As he stepped into the clearing, Ada was standing where he had left her. He hung the keg on a branch and walked past her. The horse snorted, tossed her head, and shifted her feet. She, too, was rested and ready to work.

Of the four horses on the farm, Ada was Thomas's favorite. There was a special bond between the man and beast. Thomas was gentle toward her, and the horse would respond with spirit toward his commands. With a pat on her neck and an adjustment of the hames harness, Thomas untied the plow reins and gave the haw command. Ada turned left, and the trace chains snapped taut as the plow point began to part the rich soil again.

Row after row, they turned over. Thomas's shirt had once been dry from the spring water, but it was soon clinging to his stout frame from the sweat of his body. Step after step from Thomas and Ada produced more plowed ground. The plow slipped smoothly though the soil. Occasionally the plow shook in Thomas's hands when it hit a hidden rock.

Seeing the sun high in the sky and becoming aware of his hunger, he brought the plowing to a halt. He unhitched Ada from the plow, and they made their way to the tree line at the edge of the field. He sat down and opened the cloth sack. His mother had prepared corn pone and slabs of fried meat.

Thomas consumed the food quickly so he could return to work. He gave a morsel of the meat to Lady, gave Ada a drink of water, and hooked the trace chains to the single tree attached to the plow. With a twitch of the reins, Ada was back at work again.

The plot of untouched ground became smaller and smaller. It was as if Ada sensed the completion of the task. Her steps became quicker. She pulled Thomas along so swiftly that he had to quicken his steps to keep from falling. The sun was slipping behind the distant western hill as the last furrow was completed.

Thomas left the plow at the edge of the field and unhooked the chains from the plow. He would leave the plow there overnight and bring the ground slide tomorrow to take it back to the barn. He draped the chains over the hames and started for home. They stopped at the creek for Ada to drink her fill.

When they reached the barn, Ada paused in the hallway between the four stalls. Thomas removed the hames with the chains and hung them on the pegs by the stall door. The horse collar was removed next, and as he walked past her, he reached between Ada's ears to pull the bridle from her head and he heard the bridle bit rattle against her teeth.

Ada went to her stall, and Thomas slowly climbed the lad- der to the loft. The cross slats were worn smooth from the many times they had been gripped as someone had climbed to reach the loft. Thomas threw down the usual two forks of hay. "Here is your reward for the hard work today," he said as a fork of clover hay filled the hay rack. As Ada munched on the hay, Thomas gave her a good rubdown with the curry comb. A gentle pat on the neck signaled the end of her workday.

Thomas did not know how tired Ada was, but he knew he was about to drop in his tracks. He stopped by the cistern to draw a bucket of water.

Taking the gourd dipper from the porch column, he filled it with water. Instead of drinking, he poured the cool water over his head.

Dipper after dipper he poured over his head and back. He saved the last dipper for drinking, which he put down without stopping. Leaving his boots and most of his clothes on the back porch to dry overnight, he started up the stairs to his room. He heard Ma call out that stew and corn bread were on the kitchen stove. Thomas managed a weakly reply that he was too tired to eat. He stumbled on the top step and fell toward his bed. Almost as soon as he closed his eyes, the day fell behind him.

Chapter 13

Thomas was awoke to the gentle touch of her hand.

"The sun is almost down," she reported. "You have slept the day through. It has surely done you good."

Thomas got up from the hammock. There was a little pain, but it was not unbearable.

They went inside the cabin. Abigail already had bowls of vegetables and a platter of chicken on the table.

Thomas ate as though he had not eaten in days. He did not consider that he would not hear the rooster crow on tomorrow's morn.

By the time they finished eating, it was dark outside. Abigail lit a lamp and cleared the table. When she finished, she sat down opposite Thomas. Her fair complexion and high cheekbones were the most beautiful he had ever seen with the exception of his Jenny.

She began to talk about Caleb and the sorrowful day she had watched him step off the front porch, walk down the path to the gate, and turn onto the road. She had watched him until he walked around the bend in the road.

Thomas wondered what it had been like for his Jenny as he left her on the train depot landing. She said, "I hear Noah and other men talking about how the Virginia army is keeping the Yankees out of Virginia. "So many men and boys have left our county to join the army- and so many will never come home. Why did you join in Tennessee?"

"When I joined up, the war was about keeping the Yankees out of Virginia," Thomas began. "If I had waited until now, I probably would still be in Tennessee. I received mail from my family stating the forts on the Cumberland River have fallen into the hands of the enemy and that Clarksville is occupied. Since the Yankees control the Cumberland, it won't be long before they can take Nashville- if they haven't by now. If Nashville falls, then Tennessee will soon be in the hands of the Union Army. I wish I was helping defend Tennessee soil, but maybe we are keeping Yankees out of Virginia. When my state seceded,

I felt like I should do my part." Thomas watched the lamp flame flicker. Looking at Abigail's face, he added, "Whether I am in Tennessee or here in Virginia, I think I am doing my part."

They sat in silence for a while. He returned his attention to the lamp flame. He did not realize Abigail was taking notice of his features. Abigail eventually tilted the lamp chimney to blow out the flame. She replaced it on the mantel and walked to the dogtrot door.

Thomas had been mesmerized by the flame and did not hear the door open and close. Sleep once again found his aching body for the farm.

His sleep was interrupted by the sound of wood being chopped. He was still trying to get the sleep from his eyes when Abigail appeared in the kitchen door with an armload of wood for the stove. He watched her preparing their morning meal.

After they ate, Abigail changed his bandages. "You are healing very well," she said. "The minie ball must have come from a long distance, and your thick wool coat kept it from going very deep."

Thomas still wondered which army had given him the "present." It was a gift that he certainly could have done without.

"I need to do some hoe work in my garden to stop the grass and weeds. You still need to take it easy-so don't even think about helping me."

Thomas got up from the chair as Abigail put on her work bonnet. He followed her out to the back porch, and she exchanged her moccasins for work boots. She took her hoe from its hanging spot on the porch, walked to the garden, and began hoeing.

Thomas turned his attention to the porch. It was th first time he had been out back. There was a crosscut saw and a bucksaw for cutting firewood. A washtub hung from a nail. A small kettle was turned upside down next to the wall. There was a bench to sit on when changing shoes. A plank shelf between two porch columns had pots of herbs and flowers in bloom. On a string line above, some towels were drying in the morning breeze.

Thomas stepped off the porch and into the yard. He walked past the wash kettle and the woodpile. He made his way to the barn lot fence. Big Jake was standing by the gate, lazily swishing flies with his tail. Thomas put out his hand and stroked the broad neck.

Jake tossed his head up and down.

"Thanks for bringing me here, big guy. You saved my life." Thomas scratched behind Jake's ear.

Jake tossed his head again and gave a short whinny. Thomas continued stroking and admiring the roan horse.

"You are almost as big as my Ada." Thomas gave a final pat and turned to walk away.

A large white oak tree stood in one corner of the rail-fenced yard. A wooden plank sticking out of the ground caught his eye. He walked over to it and saw that it was a grave marker: Baby Hannah, October 3, 1861-April 6, 1862. He wondered what might have happened to Caleb's and Abigail's child. He decided not to ask because he could not bear the thought of bringing sorrow to her mind.

He continued his walk around the yard. There were flowers everywhere, and there was a big snowball bush like the one at his aunt Mattie's house. He saw farm tools hanging from the side of the smokehouse. He pulled the door open and looked inside. There was a ham, some side meat, and three sacks of sausage hanging over the remains of the smoking firepit. He noted several three- and five-gallon crock jars. He supposed they might contain kraut or pickles. The saltbox for salting meat sat next to them. There were white crystals of salt at the seams and corners where it had leached through. He lingered for a while, enjoying the aroma of the atmosphere.

He left the smokehouse and walked to the barn. It was quite sturdy and had stalls for the cow and Jake. He smelled hay in the loft. A chicken startled him as she cackled, announcing the laying of her egg in the box nest nailed to the wall.

He walked outside and saw a small pond. Beyond the barn lot was a small field of corn that was up to his knee. Thomas guessed it would provide enough to feed the cow and Jake for the winter. Alongside the barn was a garden with rows of corn, beans, squash, cabbage, and pumpkins. Abigail was right. An early frost would not give some of the plants time to mature. Thomas looked around for Abigail and saw her bent-over frame hard at work.

He came to a trellis of grapes that was full of clusters of small green grapes. He saw a patch of rhubarb shoots growing from the leaves that had given them protection during the win- ter. The sight made him recall the pies Ma would make from the plants growing by their smokehouse. As Thomas surveyed all that he had seen, he knew Caleb and Abigail had a nice home- stead.

Thomas turned to walk back to the cabin, and a well- worn path caught his eye. *This must be the way to the spring.* He followed the path into the woods and came to a limestone- walled springhouse. Thomas knelt down and cupped his hands together to fill them with water. By the time he got his hands to his mouth, most of the water had leaked out between his fingers and was running down his arms to his elbows. He opened the door to look inside and saw a crock jar. Lifting the wooden top, he saw that it contained milk.

Closing the door, he stood up. His eyes fell on a dipper gourd hanging from a post. Taking the gourd, he filled it with water. The water was cool and refreshing. He drank most of a second dipper. He poured the rest over one hand and rubbed the water on his face. Returning the gourd to its hanging place, he leaned against the wall of the springhouse. As he looked up into the tree branches, he saw little diamond points of light glistening from dew drops on the leaves. He closed his eyes, and pictures of his farm and Jenny began to swirl in his *mind. Jenny, oh my sweet Jenny,* he thought.

Thomas remembered the first time he had seen her. The Blackwell family had moved into the community down the creek from their farm. He and Pa had ridden by the Blackwell place to greet the new family and to be neighborly. Thomas had not paid much attention to the barefoot girl with pigtails.

The Blackwells had come from North Carolina, and the two families soon became good friends. They began to help each other with spring planting and fall harvesting. They attended the same church and often took Sunday meals together.

Chapter 14

It was one Sunday morning as everyone left church that Thomas really noticed Jenny for the first time. He had found himself thinking about her several times since the corn shucking. He was standing outside the church as the Blackwells passed Reverend Brandon praising the sermon. In place of pigtails, there was flowing golden hair. Her bonnet was tied under her chin. The blue dress accented her attractive figure.

She had grown into quite a lovely young woman. As Jenny was about to climb onto their buggy, he tipped his hat and said, "Good day, Miss Jenny."

"Good day to you, Thomas," she said. Thomas helped her up to the buggy seat. She smiled and gave a nod of thanks.

Mr. Blackwell snapped the reins, and the buggy lurched forward.

An unexplainable feeling came over Thomas. He managed to walk to his wagon and get settled on the tailgate. He let his legs dangle from the end of the wagon, and the ride home began. He looked back and thought he caught a glimpse of Jenny quickly turning around as if she had been looking back at him.

For Thomas, the week passed slowly. He could not think of an excuse for anything needed from the Blackwell farm so that he might see Jenny. Church on Sunday could not come soon enough. Sunday finally came, and he saw Jenny again. More than once, he tried to twist around in his seat to gaze in her direction. Each time, Ma cleared her throat with the particular sound of disapproval she was noted for.

When Reverend Brandon finally finished, Thomas waited anxiously outside for Jenny to come out with the rest of her family.

Thomas summed up his courage and said, "Miss Jenny, may I walk you home?"

"Yes, but you will have to ask my father first."

Mr. Blackwell was a large man. He had a gentle disposition, but he could be quite intimidating. Thomas waited for Mr. Blackwell to finish his conversation with a group of men. "Mr. Blackwell, may I walk Jenny home from church today?"

Mr. Blackwell's eyes scanned him from his hat to his shoes. Not wanting to show intimidation, Thomas made eye contact with Mr. Blackwell.

"Yes, son. You may walk Jenny home." As Thomas turned to leave, Mr. Blackwell winked and added, "You enjoy the walk now, you hear?"

That began a regular Sunday ritual. In time, Thomas did not want to leave when he said goodbye. The summer gave way to the fall. The fall ended with the coming winter. On a spring Sunday morning, about halfway to Jenny's house, Thomas said, "Jenny, will you marry me?"

Her eyes met his, and he saw a gleam in her eyes that he had never seen before. "Yes," she replied, "but you will have to- "

"Ask your father."

They walked the rest of the way in silence. Thomas kept trying to find the words to say to her father.

When Jenny's house came into view, Thomas felt his mouth go dry. His breathing quickened, and he began to feel lightheaded. His hands were clammy with sweat. A dry mouth and wet hands only caused more confusion. He turned to speak to Jenny as they approached the gate, but the words were stuck in his throat.

Jenny said, "We'll stop by the cistern to draw a fresh dipper of water before we go into the house."

Thomas drew in a deep breath and exhaled slowly, which helped some. By the time they reached the cistern, he felt better.

The cool water helped even more. A drop of water ran down his chin from the gourd dipper.

Jenny used her handkerchief to wipe it away.

Thomas felt awkward, but the smile on Jenny's face sent a different message. He returned the gourd to its hanging place, and they started for the front porch.

Jenny leaned close and whispered, "Don't let Daddy scare you. He only puts up a big front."

Thomas was regaining his composure, and her words were very comforting. He remembered the words from Grandpa Fletcher that anything worth having was something worth fighting for. Jenny was certainly worth a fight.

They climbed the steps to the porch, and Thomas opened the door for her. He panicked slightly because her entire family was in the front room.

Jenny said, "Pa, Thomas wants to ask you something on the porch."

Mr. Blackwell did not speak as he stood up.

Thomas did not catch the wink aimed in Mrs. Blackwell's direction.

Thomas summed all the courage he had. "Mr. Blackwell, I have been walking Jenny home from church for some time now. Jenny and I have discovered we have a lot of things in common. I know how I feel about Jenny, and I think I know how she feels about me. So, to get to the point, sir, I am asking your permission to ask Jenny to marry me." Thomas felt as if a great weight was lifted, but then he realized that Mr. Blackwell's answer might not be what he wanted to hear.

Mr. Blackwell put a hand on each shoulder and replied, "Her ma and I have been noticing you two, and we are not surprised. Do you remember the kiss at the corn shucking? It has been fun watching Jenny watching you since then. I am going to answer your question by saying yes on one condition. You take good care of my little girl, you hear?"

Thomas could hardly restrain himself. He certainly didn't want to do anything foolish right off and make Mr. Blackwell wonder about his sanity. Curbing his emotions as best he could, Thomas said, "Thank you, sir."

Descending the steps, he wanted to shout, but he managed to maintain composure. As he reached the yard gate, he heard an outburst of laughter from within Jenny's house. He was almost home before he realized what the laughter was about. He had only asked Mr. Blackwell permission to ask if he could ask to marry Jenny. He had been so elated he had not asked the final question. He finally decided that the Blackwell family had gotten a good laugh at his blunder. The rest of the way home, he barely felt the dusty road beneath him.

Thomas and Jenny picked the last day of July as their wedding date. The beautiful day was full of emotion. They had only been married for a year when the call went out for more soldiers from Tennessee. Thomas had gathered promises from other family members to look out for Jenny while he was gone. He remembered kissing her for the last time at the train depot in Clarksville.

A vision of Jenny's face formed in Thomas's mind. A gust of wind swept across his face, and he could almost see it blow a wisp of Jenny's hair across her cheek. Wrapping himself in these thoughts, Thomas stretched out on the ground next to the spring. After pulling his hat down over his eyes, he fell asleep.

Chapter 15

The shrill cry of a blue jay announced an intruder. A twig cracked, and Thomas sat up.

"I thought I might find you here," Abigail said. She was coming to the spring to get a fresh bucket of water for the evening. She also had a crock jug of the evening milking to put in the springhouse.

Thomas realized he had spent the entire day beside the spring.

He got up as she filled the bucket, and they walked back to the cabin.

Abigail carried the bucket of water, and he carried the crock jug of the milk.

After supper, Abigail cleared the table and sat down across from him.

The lamp cast a glow around the room unlike any of the previous nights. Thomas felt the warmth and comfort of the cabin.

Abigail asked if he played the fiddle.

"Yes, a little- but it has been a long time since I played because of the war."

Abigail went to the mantle, retrieved the instrument, and placed it on the table in front of him.

He picked it up and began to pluck the strings, tuning it the best he could. He tightened the bow and cradled the instrument under his chin. The first few draws of the bow across the strings produced a horrible screeching sound that would have driven a ghost from its hiding place.

The sounds got better as his fingers limbered up, and the sawing motion became easier. The screeching soon became a recognizable melody. Thomas began to sway in time as he played. A smile came to his face, and he enjoyed the moment.

Abigail got up and began to dance. She twirled around lightly on her feet. She made big circles around the room, twisting and turning as she danced. Her skirt swished back and forth as she moved effortlessly. She had taken the braids from her hair, and it fluttered in the air.

He played, and she danced. She danced, and Thomas played – on and on with the tempo getting faster and faster. Just as Thomas's arm was about to give out from the vigorous playing, she slumped on the bench opposite him. She wiped her brow with the hem of her apron. They sat there for a long time. They did not speak, but they stared into each other's souls.

A feeling like no other engulfed Thomas. He had experienced it only once before, and that was when he and Jenny...

Thomas closed his eyes and swallowed hard to send the feeling from his mind. They sat a while longer. Thomas knew his wound was not quite healed, but he knew that he had to leave. He was fearful of breaking his vows to Jenny. He sensed that Abigail might not put up much resistance to an advance.

Abigail got up, took the fiddle from Thomas, and returned it to the mantel. She slowly made her way to the door, opened it, and looked back at Thomas.

They gazed at each other for a moment.

He did not move, and she finally turned and closed the door behind her.

Thomas tilted the lamp chimney and extinguished the flame. He heard the door open and close across the dogtrot.

He stretched out on the cot, adjusted the pillow under his head, and thought about Jenny. He remembered the special day he had watched Jenny walk down the aisle toward him. He closed his eyes, and the memory began to form the images of that first night. He lay in silence until sleep swallowed his thoughts.

Thomas struggled with the collar button on his shirt. It was partly due to outgrowing the shirt and the nervousness of his fumbling fingers. In a few hours, he and Jenny would be married. Ma had washed, starched, and ironed the shirt. She had altered Pa's coat down to his size.

Samuel had cleaned and buffed his boots. Almeda had sewn him a new pair of pants. Pa had given him a haircut, and he was clean-shaven. Tying his tie, he tried to anticipate his life with Jenny.

Thomas and Jenny had spent several weeks fixing up the old Jubal Adams cabin. Jubal and his family had been on their way from Virginia to Texas. The need for supplies and a broken wagon had caused them to stop in Lone Oak.

Grandpa Fletcher needed help with the farmwork, and Jubal needed a place to settle for a while. Grandpa supplied materials for Jubal to build the cabin, and Jubal worked for him. Jubal lived there until his family outgrew the modest little cabin that had been built across the creek on a spring day, Jubal loaded his family and their few possessions on his wagon and started out for Texas.

Thomas had repaired the shingle roof, replaced glass in the broken windows, and cleaned out the nearby spring. Jenny had made curtains for the windows and spent many hours cleaning. Spiderwebs filled the corners. The mud nests of dirt daubers had to be removed. Squirrels had left walnut hulls behind, and Jenny swept the dust from the upstairs loft and cleaned the floor with water.

Samuel helped replace the fallen chimney stones. They repaired the shed behind the cabin to house Ada when she ended the day's work. New rails were cut for a yard fence. Thomas plowed a small garden plot. Vegetables would come from Ma's garden, but Jenny wanted a place for flowers.

His thoughts were interrupted as Ma said, "Is everybody ready?"

They all assembled on the front porch and waited for Pa to bring the buggy up from the stable. Samuel had cleaned the dust from the horse-drawn vehicle. He had curried Ada to get rid of the last of her winter coat. Her brown coat glistened in the sunlight. Almeda picked lilac flowers and tied them to Ada's harness.

Pa climbed down from the seat and handed the reins to Thomas. "You take the buggy, and the rest of us will take the wagon. You and Jenny can leave the church in the buggy."

Thomas climbed on and sat down on the padded buggy seat. "Thank you all for making this a special day," he said. He observed the smile and tears on Ma's face. Pa pretended to be adjusting Ada's harness, but there was a tear on his cheek as well.

By the time he glanced toward Almeda, she was holding her handkerchief to her nose. Samuel was kicking a clump of grass with the toe of his right shoe. "Thank you again," Thomas ended with "Giddyapf"

Ada was in motion, the trace chains tightened, and the wheels began to turn.

He drove through the yard gate and started down the hill, passing the corn crib and horse stables. After this day, things would be quite different. The big, white clapboard house on the hill would no longer be his home. He would still be accountable to Pa for farm things, but he would now have a wife to think of- and someday a family, he hoped. He realized that his time with Samuel would be different. The trip to the church was uneventful, but his mind was flooded with memories of the things he and Samuel had done.

Chapter 16

There were several people in the church when Thomas jumped down from the buggy and hitched Ada. Jenny and her mother had decorated the church. There were bouquets of daisies and black-eyed Susans on each windowsill. At the front of the church, where they would stand during the ceremony, he saw an arbor covered with wisteria vines and hanging clusters of purple flowers.

As Thomas paced nervously up and down the aisle, there were well wishes from those present. The rest of his family eventually arrived, and they took their places in a front pew. More and more of the relatives and friends of the Lyles gathered in the little clapboard building. While the Blackwells had no close relatives, the community had become close with the family.

Thomas caught sight of William, Harry, and Jordan in the back pew. They had strange smiles on their faces. He wondered what they were up to, but he decided to think of more important things as the church door opened.

Jenny's family arrived and took their places in the other front pew. Jenny's father, mother, and two sisters acknowledged Thomas as they sat. Jenny waited outside.

At the appointed time of the ceremony, Reverend Brandon took his place under the arbor. He motioned for Thomas to join him. Thomas stood, walked to stand beside the preacher, and turned to face those who had gathered. Miss Wilma, the church pianist, began to play an unfamiliar song.

Jenny stepped through the doorway and began to walk slowly down the aisle.

Thomas was overcome with the beauty of the scene. He could not take his eyes off of her. She was wearing a long white dress with lace for the bodice. The sleeves were also lace. Thomas knew that Mrs. Blackwell had done the tatting to make the lace. Jenny carried a bouquet of wisteria and daisies. Her golden hair was braided and circled on top of her head. Jenny eventually made her way to where he was standing. As she took her place beside Thomas, she slipped her arm through his. They turned to face Reverend Brandon.

"Friends and family, we are gathered here this afternoon..."

Thomas could not keep his eyes from glancing at her. He thought back to the first time he saw the barefoot, pigtailed girl. He remembered the embarrassment he had felt at the corn shucking when he kissed her. His thoughts were interrupted by the touch on his arm. From Reverend Brandon's look, Thomas realized he was supposed to say, "I do."

Looking at Jenny, he struggled to get the words past the lump in his throat. The service proceeded, but the words failed to register with Thomas. He again realized that Reverend Brandon wanted his attention. The ring - he wants the ring, thought Thomas.

He reached into his coat pocket to retrieve the ring. His fingers closed around the ring, which he had made from the silver dollar Mr. Blackwell had given him for winning the shucking contest. He looked at the ring before he gave it up.

He thought about the work he had put into making the object. He had used the bowl of a spoon to flare the edges of the coin into a wide band. He had used his pocketknife to cut away the center to make the hole for Jenny's finger. He had carefully trimmed the inside hole so there would be no sharp points. He had guessed about how large to make the hole. He had not wanted to make it too large for Jenny's finger. If it were too small, he could always trim it larger after they were married.

He heard his pastor say something, and the ring was placed in his hand again. He took Jenny's hand and placed the ring on her finger.

"I pronounce you man and wife. You may kiss your bride."

Thomas placed his hands on her cheeks, which were wet with tears, and drew her face closer. The kiss was so much more than their first kiss. They held the kiss for a respectful time and ended with an embrace under the perfumed air of the wisteria blossoms.

Thomas and Jenny walked the aisle to the door of the church and greeted those who had come to the service. When everyone was gone except for their families, Mr. Blackwell shook Thomas's hand and said, "Well, I finally got a son. All the women at my house drive me crazy sometimes."

Mrs. Blackwell hugged them both at once. "Welcome to our family, Thomas. May you have many years of happiness."

Jenny's younger sisters embraced her and giggled as they passed Thomas.

Jenny said, "Now you and Samuel have two more sisters." Samuel noted that one sister was enough.

Reaching the bottom step, Mr. Blackwell turned and said, "Thomas, remember what I told on the front porch now, you hear?"

Thomas smiled. "I promise I will. I promise I will." He looked at Jenny and saw a puzzled look on her face. "I'll tell you sometime," he said.

It was then time for the Lyle family to offer their best wishes.

Almeda hugged Jenny. "I am so glad to finally have a sister. Just having two brothers is no fun." She let go of her embrace with Jenny and turned to Thomas. "I love you," she said as she kissed his cheek.

Thomas put his arms around Almeda and thought about some of the tricks he had done to her. He let go of the embrace and placed his hands on her shoulders. "I love you too, and I am sorry for some of the tricks I played on you."

They both had a good laugh as Almeda stepped to the doorway.

Ma gave Jenny a hug and said, "It's good to have another daughter in the family." She placed a hand on Thomas's shoulder. "You be a good husband and-in time-a good father."

He extended his arms to give her a hug. "If I could be like Pa..." The words stuck in his throat, and he could not finish the sentence.

Pa embraced them both and drew them close together. "We are glad to have you in the family, Jenny. Thomas, I think you have made a very good choice for a wife."

Jenny kissed him on the cheek and said, "I promise to be a good wife for Thomas."

Samuel had been lingering by the last pew, and he stepped to face Jenny and Thomas. There was a long moment of silence between the three of them.

Thomas knew that most of his time would involve taking care of his domestic responsibilities, but he would still need to do things with his brother.

Samuel said, "You are a lucky man. I hope I can find someone like Jenny to be my wife someday. I have known since the corn shucking that you and Jenny would get married someday." He reached out to embrace Jenny. He turned to Thomas, and the embrace became a back-slapping bear hug.

Samuel descended the church steps. Neither brother saw the tears on the other's cheeks.

Thomas turned his attention to Jenny.

They looked at each other for a moment and whispered, "I love you."

Thomas took Jenny by the hand and led her down the church steps. They walked arm in arm to the buggy. Thomas patted the big horse's neck and said, "You have someone else to take care of now, big girl."

Ada tossed her head and snorted. Thomas helped Jenny up to the buggy seat. She slid over to make room for Thomas. He untied the reins from the brake pole and said, "Let's go, girl!"

Ada stepped forward, tightening the trace chains, and the buggy lurched into motion.

Jenny rested her head against Thomas's shoulder. He slipped an arm around her and pulled her close. They rode in silence until Thomas let out a chuckle.

"What is it?" Jenny asked.

"I was just thinking about all those times we walked down this road to your house. Now we are riding to our home."

Chapter 17

When they arrived at their cabin, Thomas quickly jumped down to hitch Ada. He walked around to Jenny's side to help her down. She stood to let him reach up to her. He lifted her and let her slender waist slide through his hands as he set her on the ground. Taking her hand, he led her across the yard, up the steps, and to the front door.

Thomas turned to Jenny, slipped his arm around her waist, and drew her close to him. He buried his face in her hair, which she had let down on the ride home. "I've waited so long for this moment. I love you, and I promise to work hard and someday give you a better house. I will-"

She placed a finger on his lips. "We will work together to make this our home and raise our family."

Thomas straightened himself up to look into her eyes. "Oh, Thomas. I promise to be a good wife for you."

They gazed at each other for a moment. A tear began to trickle down her cheek. He wiped it away with a finger and kissed her cheek.

He lifted the door latch and pushed the door aside. When they stepped inside, they were surprised to find their table covered with food.

"Our wedding supper," Jenny exclaimed. There was a platter of fried ham, a bowl of hominy, poke salad greens, and a bowl of boiled potatoes that Thomas guessed were the last remnants of the previous year's crop. Beside the plate of corn pone was butter and milk from the springhouse. To top it all off was Jenny's mother's molasses pie.

They ate mostly in silence. It was the first time either had been alone with the opposite gender in such a private setting. The tension was partially lifted when Thomas passed his plate for a piece of pie and his fork fell into the bowl of potatoes. They both had a laugh and finished their supper.

Thomas pushed back from the table and said, "I am going to put Ada in the shed and feed her." Thomas walked down the front porch steps and paused to look around. He allowed himself sometime of reflection as he looked back at the cabin. For a moment, he was full of fear and pride.

The day had changed his life. He now had new responsibilities, but he knew he could deal with the challenges he would face. He believed he would be able to meet his farm responsibilities while being a good husband to Jenny.

He made his way across the yard to the hitching post. He unhooked the trace chain from the buggy and hung them. He led Ada to her stall. "I know this is not as good as the big stable, but give me some time, and I will build you a better barn." He made a trip to the spring to bring water for the water trough and gave Ada a currying as she munched on her hay.

Dusk had set in by the time he finished settling Ada for the night. As he returned to the cabin, he observed the glow of a lamp coming through the front window. He pushed the door open, and the scene he observed brought a wave of emotions like none he had ever experienced.

Jenny had turned down the bedcovers and was sitting on the foot of the bed. She had removed the flowers and braids from her hair, and it spilled across her shoulders. She stood up to greet Thomas and stepping in front of the lamp caused a shadow to fall on the floor toward him. Her body inside the white gown was silhouetted by the backlight.

Thomas saw the shadows and curves of her youthful figure. The floor shadow was like a pathway leading him to her. Words were not necessary. He moved anxiously but cautiously toward her. He took her into his arms. The kisses were short at first, little more than short, light touches of the lips. The kisses gradually got longer and deeper. Thomas moved his hands around to explore the softness of her body.

Jenny pulled his shirt from Thomas's pants and began to unbutton it from the bottom up. When she finished with the last button, she pushed the collar across his broad shoulders.

He unbuttoned the cuff buttons and let the shirt slide from his arms. The shirt fell to the floor.

The embraces and kisses became even more intense. Jenny slipped from his arms and turned the lamp wick down to just a soft glow. As she turned to face Thomas, she untied the bowstrings at the bodice of her gown.

Thomas pushed the gown aside to reveal her bare shoulders. He made several passes of his fingertips between her shoulder and neck. He slowly pushed the gown off her shoulders and down to reveal her bare arms.

Jenny pulled her hands from the sleeves, and the garment fell to the floor.

Thomas picked her up tenderly and laid her on the bed. He finished undressing and lay down beside her. Passion of all passions ensued as they embraced and explored each other's bodies. The night eventually became their blanket, and they fell asleep entwined in an embrace.

Both were suddenly awakened by a horrendous clamor outside. Startled, they sat up in bed. It took a moment for Thomas to gain his senses from the interrupted deep sleep.

"What is going on? 'Jenny pulled the covers around herself.

The clamor continued, and Lady joined in the commotion. "It's a shivaree" Thomas replied with obvious disgust in his voice. He jumped from the bed and started for the door. "Thomas, you don't have any clothes on," Jenny said.

"It won't matter if it's who I think it is," Thomas said as he reached for the door latch.

Lady could be heard barking and growling. He threw open the door and stepped onto the porch.

The clamor ended as Lady jumped to the ground. She chased three figures from the yard and through the gate. There wasn't much moonlight, but he recognized the trio. He laughed as he watched Lady chasing them across the hayfield, barking and nipping at the heels of those causing the ruckus.

Chapter 18

Thomas woke up the smell of side meat frying and biscuits baking.

Abigail said, "Morning. I packed your haversack with meat and bread, and your canteen is full of fresh water." The tone of her voice and the look on her face gave Thomas the message that she also realized it was time for him to be on his way.

When he finished eating, he stood up and draped his canteen and haversack over his shoulder. "I have something else for you. Here is your yankee present," she said as she placed the minie ball in his palm.

Her fingers curled around his as she pressed his fingers against the object. He stared at it and knew that it would remind him of the days spent in her presence. Thomas' heart fluttered in his chest. The minie ball was not round. It was a Union ball. He had been running the wrong way! The thought stunned him for a moment.

"What's wrong?" she asked.

"This is a Yankee bullet. I thought I was shot by one of my own men. The ordnance we were using was the round ball shot." He turned the lead object over and over again. "This is a Yankee ball." He closed his eyes in relief. Turning to face her, he said, "I will never forget you, Abigail McAllister, and my Jenny will thank you for your kindness also." He wanted to embrace her in thanks, but he decided against the gesture.

He turned and walked across the room to the porch door. He opened the door, crossed the porch, stepped down to the rock slab step, and started down the path to the yard gate. When he reached the gate, he turned to gaze at Abigail one last time. He was too far away to see the tears on her cheek. He lifted his hand to tug on his hat brim to acknowledge her presence on the porch.

He started down the road, and not being able to look back, he raised his arm to wave over his shoulder.

"God speed, Thomas Lyle!" he heard her shout.

Tears began to well up in his eyes. His being was overtaken by thankfulness and sorrow. He was thankful that he had found someone to care for him and that his wound was healing from her care. He was sorrowful about leaving on her presence. He knew he should not think of her in that way, but if he had not been married to Jenny and she had not married to Caleb, he would have liked to have been able to have called Abigail his wife.

He could not imagine any two women being more compassionate than his Jenny and Abigail. He had experienced unforgettable tenderness from Abigail. The farm would have been a great place to live. He began to imagine raising a family with her.

When he realized the thoughts, he was having, his conscience began to shame him. "I am sorry, Jenny. Forgive me. I could never forsake my vows to you. I love you. I love you, I love you!" He sank to his knees on the dusty road.

After a while, he regained his composure. He collected his canteen and haversack, removed his hat, and wiped at the dust on his pants. Putting his hat back on, he set his eye on the road.

The long shadows pointing westward told Thomas it was early morning. Before long, he came to the little creek. He saw a reddish-brown patch of sand on the riverbank. He stared at it, knowing his blood had left the stain.

He waded to the other side and quickened his steps, trying to put the place behind him and out of his memory. The morning went by quickly, and his brisk gait caused him to sweat. Removing his patched coat, he threw it over his shoulder. He paused long enough to wash the dust from his throat by taking a sip of water from the canteen. He did not know where he was going, but he figured he would run into the war somewhere.

The road eventually began to follow the bank of a larger creek. Thomas felt the cool atmosphere coming from the clear water as it gurgled over the rocks. It reminded him of the creek running through the farm back home.

The shadows had become much shorter, and he found a large sycamore tree to rest under by a large pool of water. There were some small daisy-like flowers growing near him. Thomas pulled a handful of the blossoms from their stems.

He tossed one into the pool. Before he could toss a second one, the first was swallowed by a large bass that made a big splash as it broke the water's surface. He tossed the second and a third, and each flower was swallowed in a flourish as the large fish took the meal. He leaned back against the tree, opened his haversack, and took out some of the food Abagail had packed for him. As he began to eat, the sounds of the creek reminded him of an afternoon back on the farm when Almeda had played a trick on her brothers. Though he had never been able to get Almeda to admit it, he was sure she had been the one to do the deed.

"Yank your line-the float has gone under," Samuel yelled.

Thomas and Samuel had finished hoeing the cornfield and had decided to do some fishing at the ford. The ford had been named such by grandpa Fletcher where the Stuart and Hurricane Creeks merged. The swirling water often washed out a rather large pool. A large rock slab about ten feet up on the creek bank made a good place to fish and swim.

Thomas pulled on his line and felt the tug of the fish as it tried to run downstream. For a moment, it felt like he had hooked a big one, but his line suddenly went limp. "Oh, no- he got away." Thomas began to twist his pole to wind the line up and put new bait on the hook.

He was about to put a big white grubworm on his hook. "You know, Samuel, we have been fishing for a long time, and we have not caught a thing. Let's take off our clothes and go swimming. We'll have more fun doing that. Besides, I am tired of catching nothing."

Off came the shoes, socks, pants, shirts, and long johns. They pitched their clothes up the bank and shouted, "Last one in is a rotten egg!"

They were enjoying splashing water on each other, dunking heads, and climbing up the rock slab to grab the rope tied to the cottonwood tree branch. A running start would propel the rider out over the pool for a nice drop into the water. The noise from the splashing and shouting filled the woods.

Almeda and her friend Bernice were walking home from the store. The shortcut through the woods led the two girls close to the ford. Almeda was usually a serious person, not given to a lot of practical jokes. However, she had been trying to figure out what she could do to Thomas for the frog he had put under her bedcovers one night.

Of course, Thomas had a most innocent expression and absolutely did not know how a frog could have made its way into her bed. When Thomas suggested that she kiss it and maybe a prince would appear, Almeda threw a pillow at him. Instead of hitting Thomas, the pillow knocked a chimney from a lamp. The lamp chimney had broken into a dozen pieces when it hit the floor. Almeda's punishment was to buy another chimney from the general store.

Almeda and Bernice heard the shouting at the fishing hole. Almeda knew it was Thomas and Samuel. The girls crept through the underbrush and watched Thomas and Samuel splashing in the water. The girls had to put their hands over their mouths to snuff out giggles from seeing the boys without clothes.

Almeda found a long stick and pushed it toward the boys' clothes. Garment by garment, the clothes came into the possession of Almeda. The two girls silently slipped through the bushes and back to the main path. When they reached the path, they gave in and laughed out loud.

The girls had all the boys' clothes except their shoes, and Almeda had finally gotten even with Thomas.

They soon reached the path that led to Bernice's house.

Almeda took the clothes and continued homeward. When she reached home, she neatly folded the clothes and left them on the back porch bench.

The water fun came to an end, and Thomas and Samuel climbed to the bank where they had left their clothes.

"What happened to our clothes?" Samuel asked. Thomas said, "Well, at least we have our shoes." "But... but ... we can't walk home naked."

The boys continued to search the bushes.

"What are we going to do?" Samuel asked.

Thomas slipped on his shoes and made his way toward a basswood tree. It would not take many branches of the large, round leaves to cover their vital areas. They soon had enough leaves to cover themselves and started homeward.

"I would like to know what happened to our clothes," Samuel said.

"I think somebody is playing a trick on us," Thomas said. "I am sure it wasn't some animal that took our clothes and left our shoes."

"I sure hope nobody sees us," Samuel said. "I am not Adam, and you certainly are not Eve."

The two leaf-covered boys were trying to walk as fast as possible. They were constantly turning around to see if anyone was approaching from behind.

"I feel like the woods are full of people," Samuel said.

"I don't think the animals care," Thomas replied. "Wait! I hear something coming down the road."

They heard jingling trace chains, the rumble of a wagon, and shouts admonishing a team of animals to go faster.

"Guess who," said Samuel. "The Johnsons," Thomas said.

"We can't let them see us like this. We would never hear the end of it." Samuel started for the woods.

"Thank goodness for the woods. A little further down the road-and we would have been in an open field without any cover," Thomas said.

They made their way into the woods, and the wagon rum- bled past. Asa Johnson was shouting, popping his whip, and pushing his team of mules beyond reason.

"I feel sorry for their animals," Samuel said.

"Yeah, I would never run Ada that way," Thomas said.

They waited for the wagon to disappear around the bend and made their way back to the road. They paused briefly to listen for other travelers. The only things they heard were the chirpings of the birds.

The rest of the way home was uneventful. As they neared their house, they stopped to hide behind the smokehouse to spy out the back porch and the yard.

"Look on the porch bench," Samuel exclaimed. "Our clothes. I'll make a run for them and bring them back for us. We can leave the tree branches here and walk across the yard as though nothing has happened." He ran to the porch.

Lady, in her usual spot, did not respond to him.

Clothes gathered, Samuel leaped from the porch and ran for the cover of the smokehouse. The plan worked, and they were soon doing the nighttime chores.

"If Lady had been with us, our clothes would not have been taken," Thomas said.

Lady had followed them to the cornfield. After watching Thomas work for a while, she had picked up the scent of something and run off in search of the mystery odor.

After washing up at the cistern, Thomas and Samuel sat down on the back porch and waited for Ma's call to supper.

Lady sat down in front of Thomas and held up a paw.

He had taught her to shake hands, and she never seemed to grow tired of the trick.

After playing with her for a while, Thomas picked up her knotted rope and threw it into the yard.

Lady immediately ran to retrieve it and brought it back to Thomas. She dropped it in front of him, sat down, and waited for him to pick it up.

Ma called for everyone to come to the table.

After Pa blessed the food, he said, "You boys finish with the cornfield?"

"Yes, sir," replied Thomas.

"What did you do when you got through?" Pa asked. "We went fishing at the ford," Samuel said.

"Did you catch anything?" Almeda asked, and the look on her face told Thomas who the trickster was.

"No," Thomas said as he put another biscuit on his plate. "When I came by the smokehouse, I saw a bunch of bass wood branches on the ground," Pa said between bites.

Samuel and Thomas busied themselves with their plates of food.

Almeda said, "Maybe someone was playing in the Garden of Eden."

"I sometimes think this place is next to paradise, but I wouldn't consider it Eden," Ma responded.

Pa let the conversation drop and asked for a spoon of Ma's cobbler.

Chapter 19

The food and water refreshed him, and after a short rest, Thomas got up and resumed his walk. His walk followed the winding creek. When the shadows began to stretch eastward, Thomas knew the day was waning. As he rounded a bend, he saw a valley that the road crossed. His eye followed the road across the valley to where it disappeared into trees at the base of a mountain.

Thomas had walked a short distance into the valley when he saw a cloud of dust rising from the trees. It must be a column of men on the march. Are they Union or Confederate? Thomas quickly sought cover in a thicket of bushes.

He waited nervously and heard the rumble of caisson and wagon wheels and the unmistakable sound of marching feet. He spotted a battle flag as the column moved out of cover on the valley floor. He did not recognize the company or the regiment of the flag.

He broke a few more branches and stuck them in front of his hiding place for more protection. Closer and closer they came. He could hear the clanking of their accoutrements and the voices of the men.

After some anxious moments, the column got close enough -and he recognized the troops were of the Southern cause. His spirits soared, and he slipped out of his hiding place. Thomas waved his arms over his head and called out to the soldiers. An officer on horseback shouted for him to fall in line.

Thomas tried to explain who he was and what army he was with, so they would not consider him a deserter.

The officer told him to fall in line with the column. They seemed like they were in a hurry. He found an open spot and fell in with the group.

They marched in silence for a while. Thomas finally spoke to the fellow on his right. "I'm Sergeant Thomas Lyle from Company B of the Tennessee Fourteenth. I was wounded and got separated from my unit a few days ago. I figured I would eventually find somebody to join up with."

"I'm Ezra Williams, was the reply. "We are the Virginia Tenth, and we are on the way to Harpers Ferry. We are going after the supplies stored there."

They walked on, and Thomas spoke of the action he had seen. Ezra and some of the others related their stories. Ezra asked what hospital company had cared for him.

"I wasn't in a hospital. A lady took me in and doctored me." Suddenly Thomas realized he was retracing his steps of the day. He was on the way back to Abigail's farm. He told them they would pass the house in a few hours.

An officer rode by and shouted for everyone to pick up the pace. For many miles, there was less talking and more concentration on marching.

The sun slipped silently behind the distant mountains. The moon began to rise in the cloudless sky, and onward they marched. Thomas began to anticipate going by Abigail's cabin. He felt his steps quicken.

The march carried them onward, and within another hour, they reached the creek. "There is where I fell," Thomas said. The creek bank was in a shadow, so the blood-stained earth was not visible. "Just up this road is the McAllister farm. A lady named Abigail patched me up."

Ezra's jaw dropped, and his eyes widened. "You're wrong there, mister. Ain't much left of the McAllister place after the Yankees done went and burnt it last year."

Thomas was stunned. "I know better. I just spent three days at the farm. Abigail dressed my wound, and she dug this Yankee minie ball out of me."

Thomas took out the lead object. "She cooked, washed and patched my clothes, and danced when I played the fiddle. I rode her horse from here to their cabin."

Ezra shook his head. "Mister, you is plum loco. We have marched along this road several times, and we have gone by the place each time. Here, let me prove it to you." Ezra turned to look back into the ranks behind them. "Isaiah, come here."

A short, stocky fellow approached.

"Tell this fellow there ain't much left of the McAllister place," Ezra said.

Isiah looked at Thomas and said, "Mister, I don't know where you think you have been, but you ain't been at the Mc- Allister cabin. I'm from three farms over, and I know about the McAllisters."

"Caleb was killed at Manassas," Isaiah continued. "The Yankees done came through last spring and looted the place and set fire to it. My uncle Josiah has a farm over that ridge, and my uncle Noah has a farm over this way."

"Here's what I know," Isaiah said. "My wife wrote to me that neighbors saw smoke rising and went to see what was burning. By the time they got to Caleb's place, it was mostly a pile of ashes. Abigail and the baby were found out in the yard, and both were dead from their burns. My uncles buried them under a tree in the corner of the yard.

Thomas stared blankly as he heard the words. It cannot be so. It just cannot be so. "She cooked for me. She danced when I played the fiddle, she ... she took this ball out of me."

Thomas was brought back to his senses with a shove from behind and a gruff admonishment to move on. He picked up the pace as he returned the one thing he was sure of to his pocket. He was aware of pain in his side as a result of the shove he had received. It felt like he had been completely run through by a bayonet.

As he walked beside Ezra, he kept thinking about what he had heard. *You will see that I am right, and you are wrong.* The warmth of the cabin, the touch of her hand, and his walk around the farm were things he was sure he had experienced.

The march continued. Thomas's steps were automatic, and he found himself in a daze. He eventually saw the oak tree, and he quickened his steps. Excitement boiled within him. He broke rank and ran toward the familiar sight.

"Where are you going in such a hurry?" "We'll git thar soon 'nuf!"

Being weak and getting winded, he slowed to a brisk walk. The oak tree became larger, and he eventually he reached the yard gate. As he leaned against the gate post, he did not notice the gate was only attached by one hinge. He ran to the rock step slab and stepped upon it. The color drained from his face.

Chapter 20

All that was before him were a few charred ends of logs and planks sticking up between last summer's growth of weeds. The chimney still stood, but there was nothing left but desolation. A great sweat popped out on his brow, and a chill ran up his back.

He stood there on the rock step and turned to survey the surroundings. The door to the smokehouse was hanging by the bottom hinge. The opening produced a dark gaping hole on the front of the structure. The barn was still standing, though it was missing part of the roof.

A few cornstalks could be seen above the weeds and grass because of the lack of hoeing. He turned to look toward the corner of the yard where the big oak tree grew. In the moonlight, he saw two markers under the tree. He stepped down from the rock and ran to the tree.

The markers were partially burned planks. He pulled a candle from his haversack and lit the wick. In the flickering light on the smaller plank was carved "Baby Hannah October 3, 1861- April 6, 1862. He looked at the larger marker: "Abigail McAllister August 15, 183 7- April 6, 1862." Hot wax running down the candle and onto his fingers brought him back to reality.

He blew out the flame and hastily dropped the candle in his haversack. He shoved his hands in his pockets, and his fingers closed around the minie ball, his Yankee present. He thought he heard the tinkling of a cowbell and the snorting of a horse. He turned toward the barn lot. The bright moonlight revealed nothing.

He turned back to face the charred boards. It wasn't as if he expected to see a different scene, but he had hoped he could make more sense of what he was seeing. It took his last bit of consciousness to make him realize he was not in a dream. Every now and then, a cloud would cover the moon, creating shadows that added to his confusion.

He gazed in the direction of the jumbled remains of the cabin. He replayed the past few days in his mind. He could feel Abigail's hands at his side as she took out the bullet and dressed his wound. He felt her fingers close around his as she placed the lead present in his palm.

They sat at the table, ate, and talked about their families. He played the fiddle while she danced around the room. He mar- veled at her quick feet as she spun around, causing her dress to unfurl. Her golden hair wrapped around her neck as she tossed her head.

His grandmother had told of instances where certain things could not be explained by those who had experienced un- usual circumstances. No matter what might be said about what had happened, Thomas knew it had been real. His grandmother believed that heaven provided special provisions for those in need. He had not put much thought into such philosophy before, but now he believed she was right.

As he looked at the remains of the cabin and the grave- sites, he realized the truth of her words. He had been in definite need of medical assistance, a place to recover, food, and companionship to drive away the loneliness. He wondered how long he might have been in the creek. Without treatment, gangrene could have set up in the wound.

He shuddered at the thought of being taken prisoner by the insidious Yankees. A great feeling of awe swept over him as he thought about the past three days. The surreal moment was answered as his fingers closed around the minie ball in his pocket. He made a fist around his Yankee present.

The term exploded in his brain. Abigail had given him those words. There was no doubt that all those things had happened to him. Would he have a story to tell his grandmother and the rest of the family when the war was over?

Thomas realized he had been left behind. He ran to the yard gate and picked up his canteen and haversack. He paused and turned to survey the scene one more time. A vision of the smokehouse, the barn, the tree, and the cabin filled his brain as he had seen them days before. He ran to the road without looking back.

Everyone was far ahead of him, and he set a double-quick pace to catch up. From the distant sounds, Thomas surmised he was at least a half mile behind the last man and perhaps that much more to catch up with Ezra and Isaiah.

As he hurried along, Thomas was not sure he wanted to catch up to them. Ezra was the only one he knew, but he decided to join the column with the newfound companions anyway. It took the better part of an hour to fall in step beside Ezra.

The march wore on. Fatigue began to overcome Thomas. He had spent a great deal of physical strength trying catch up. His mental state had been shocked also. Over and over, he had replayed the scenes in his mind.

Thomas realized his left shoulder was beginning to hurt from the weight of his haversack. He switched the bundle to the right shoulder. As he was making the change, he remembered he still had some jowl and biscuits that Abigail had packed for him. He wanted to tell Ezra that Abigail had cooked the meat and biscuits as he reached in to retrieve the food, but he did not feel like arguing with Ezra.

The food only served to confirm to him what had happened. The food and water did much to revitalize him. The moon slowly slid behind the distant mountains. Their eyes became accustomed the darkness as the march continued.

The sky soon began to lighten, and the darkness was pushed aside as the sun began to rise. The march continued, and orders were given to pick up the pace. Thomas learned that the Virginia Tenth had been on the march for two days before he came upon them.

That afternoon, orders were given to halt and make camp. Having exhausted the food Abigail had prepared, Thomas sought out a supply wagon.

Drawing a ration portion, he found Ezra and sat by a fire to cook the issued fare.

An officer making his inspection of the troops rode by, and Thomas got to explain who he was that he was under General A. P. Hill.

"General Hill had a victory a few days ago at Shepherdstown. We are waiting here to join him to move against Harpers Ferry. You will get to join up with your command."

The news of the victory excited Thomas. The battle he had gotten lost from had been a Southern victory. Thomas was relieved to get back with those he knew. He had gotten to know Ezra and Isiah better, but he wanted to be back with Will Harris and the others he knew best.

With food and rest, Thomas began to feel better. He re- ported to the medical tent and was advised that his wound was healing nicely.

"Where were you treated?" the medical officer asked.

"I was treated... by a lady." He really did not want to relate the story again.

The medical officer was very busy and did not press for more explanation.

Chapter 21

Mail's here!" someone called out.

Thomas crawled out of his tent to see at least twenty supply wagons approaching. Much-needed food, blankets, shoes, and packages and mail from home were on board. A supply officer would be in charge of distributing the clothing. Thomas needed new shoes, but his first stop would be the quartermaster with the mail.

The men waited for their names to be called. Thomas anxiously strained to hear his name. Shouts of joy were given up as the troops received letters and packages. Thomas was beside himself as he anticipated what he might receive.

"Sergeant Thomas Lyle," the quartermaster called out.

After shouting that he was present, he made his way through the crowd. Someone placed a package in his hands, and it was hard to contain his excitement. He made his way back to his tent, and his trembling hands tugged at the strings securing the package.

Getting all the knots untied, he ripped aside the paper: three pairs of socks, a pair of gloves, a letter, and a paper- wrapped package. The second package held tea cake cookies from Ma. He put all but three in his haversack and took the letter outside the tent. He sat under a tree and read the news from home. The cookie was hard and stale, but it was still better than anything else he had recently eaten. He munched slowly and read Jenny's letter.

Dear Thomas,

I love you, and we all wish you were here at home to see little Thomas. He is almost three months old, and even my mother says he looks like a small you. I tell him about his poppa every day. He is a good baby and doesn't cry much. I can't wait for you to see and hold him.

Pa, Samuel, and my father have worked together to get the corn crops out for both farms. Your sow had seven piglets. Lady went off somewhere and came back limping with a hurt leg, which Ma has been doctoring.

The hay is growing, and the garden has been planted.

The more he read, the more he longed to be back on the farm. He closed his eyes and tried to keep back the tears, but it was a losing battle. After a moment, he brushed away the tears on his cheeks and continued to read.

The hay is growing, the garden has been planted, and your Ma and I are making soap from the last of the hog cracklins. I hope the tea cakes are not too stale by the time they get to you. I cracked the hickory nuts that Ma put in them. I got your last letter yesterday, and I have practically worn it out reading it. My mother said she is going to send you a package soon. I rode with Pa to the general store yesterday. Mr. Edwards, Dr. Ross, and even Mrs. Johnson asked me to tell you they wished you well. We also saw Rufus Crabtree...

The name turned Thomas's thoughts sour. Rufus Crabtree had moved to Montgomery County from Ohio. When Tennessee seceded, he appointed himself "a concerned citizen helping the families south of the Cumberland River." He roamed the com- munities and claimed he was looking out for families whose men had joined Confederate forces. Most people suspected he might be doing some spying for the North. He had done small things for some families and expected some type of payment: food for himself or his horses. For families who refused his advances, something usually happened that needed fixing-and he was always willing to fix it. Rufus had paid a visit to the farm a few months ago, and the mention of his name brought back Thomas's anger.

We also saw Rufus Crabtree, and he wanted to know where in Virginia you are. Of course, we told him nothing. We pray each Sunday for everyone in our church who has joined the Southern cause. I pray for you every day. I pray that you can come home soon even if you must return to the war. We all long to see you. Take care of yourself until I write again. I gave little Thomas a kiss and told him it was from you.

Your loving Jenny

"Rufus," Thomas spat out the name, leaned against the tree, and closed his eyes. His thoughts carried him back to that afternoon.

Chapter 22

Thomas paused to wipe sweat from his brow before it trickled down into his eyes. He had been at work all afternoon in the woodworking shop. He had blisters on both hands from using the draw knife and rasps as he changed nondescript pieces of wood into useful products.

There was always a supply of wood under the workbench for making handles, shingles, or other things for the farm. He had used the froe to split out a stack of shingles from the seasoned red oak blocks. He had made a sledgehammer handle and was working on the second single tree from some two-year seasoned hickory. The shop hammer handle was also cracked and needed to be replaced. It always seemed that things broke at the most inopportune time.

He was leaving on Monday with some volunteers from Lone Oak and Palmyra to enlist in Clarksville. He was making some spares of things so Pa and Samuel could replace anything that broke.

Lady was watching Thomas work from the doorway. From time to time, she would cock her head to one side or lift an ear.

Thomas whistled as he worked, and the pile of shavings grew higher as the single tree took shape.

Suddenly Lady jumped up and growled.

Thomas put down the draw knife and started for the door. Lady never growled unless she sensed danger. "What's wrong, girl?" As he reached the doorway, he heard the rumble of wagon wheels and the jingle of the trace chains. The horse hooves grew louder as the visitors came up the hill.

Thomas glanced toward the smokehouse where Ma was preparing a kettle of hot water for washing clothes. "Who is it?" she asked.

Thomas looked down the hill. "It's Crabtree."

Rufus and his three cronies usually caused more confusion and problems than they solved.

"My Lord, what do they want?" Ma said with disgust in her voice.

Lady trotted up to Thomas. Her tail was still, and the hair on her back bristled.

Ma dropped the last of the clothes into the kettle and walked back to the porch.

She was hard to rile up, but she didn't take to folks like Crabtree. Thomas knew she had positioned herself close to what rested above the kitchen door.

"Evening, folks." was the greeting. Crabtree spit a brown stream of tobacco spittle from between a toothless grin.

"What do you want?" asked Thomas. "Oh, this is jest a social call."

"We are doing just fine-no thanks to you," Ma said.

The three riders with Crabtree dismounted and started to walk around the yard.

"What do you want?" Ma asked a second time.

"Now don't git riled up, ma'am." Crabtree shifted on the wagon seat. "With so many menfolk gone to the war, somebody has got to look out fer the folks left behind. By the way, I understand that nobody from your family has volunteered yet. We still need supplies from everyone so we can look out for everyone else. By the way, where's the rest of your menfolk?"

"Pa and Samuel are walking the line fence, making repairs-not that it is any of your business." Thomas took a step to- ward the wagon.

The Yankee Present ✻ 171

"For your information, we finished getting out our corn crop yesterday, and I am working on some things Pa and Samuel won't have to do. I am leaving next Monday to go to Clarksville to sign up. I will be going to Camp Duncan."

"Well, well, dat's news," Crabtree said. "We jess need some supplies an' we'll be on our way. You know, it's the duty of everybody to help us help each other. Leroy, check the smokehouse."

As Leroy started for the smokehouse, Lady let out a low growl.

Thomas reached for her collar and caught Ma's eye. The look, the wrinkled forehead, and the slight turn of her head told Thomas not to do anything.

After a brief disappearance, Leroy reappeared with a side of bacon and a two-gallon crock jar.

"What's in the crock?" Crabtree asked. "It's pickles."

"Oh, we's gonna have some fine eatin' there. Is them some of them pickles you won a ribbon on at last year's picnic?"

Ma didn't offer a response.

Thomas walked to the back porch "What gives you the right to go around stealing things from working folks?"

Lady stayed between Crabtree and her master.

"Now, now. We's ain't stealing. We's just appropriating. If we was stealing, we would have came over in the middle of the night."

"And you might have been shot at."

The remark caught everyone by surprise.

Pa and Samuel appeared from behind the tool shed. "Take what you took and get off our place," Pa said.

Crabtree waved his arm, and Leroy loaded the jar of pickles and meat on the wagon and mounted his horse. Crabtree slapped the rump of his horses with the reins, and the wagon was in motion. As the pillagers rode off, Crabtree yelled over his shoulder, "We's gonna stop by your stables and git some hay for our horses. They's got to eat too."

Thomas wanted to go after Crabtree and yank him from the wagon, but Pa put a hand on his shoulder and said, "Easy."

Thomas and Samuel walked toward the corn crib and watched the "appropriating." They all watched the loading of some hay and a bushel of corn.

Lady continued to growl.

When the loading was complete, Crabtree turned and gave a tug of his hat. If the move was supposed to be a thank you, Thomas viewed it as a very inadequate gesture.

Samuel, Thomas, and Lady watched as the wagon and the riders crossed the creek and started toward Lone Oak.

Chapter 23

Pa and Samuel gathered the corn and stored it in the corn crib for the winter. They had six wagonloads of pumpkins to feed the hogs. Samuel had hulled three bushels of walnuts he had gathered from the walnut tree behind the smokehouse.

Pa was getting the saltbox and scalding pan ready for the upcoming hog killing. Between the Lyles and Blackwells, there would be six hogs to kill. The hams, shoulders, bacon sides, and jowls would be salted down. The meat trimmings would be made into sausage. The fat portions would be cooked down, and the hot liquid would be put into the lard tins. Anything else would be pickled into souse.

Almeda had helped Pa make apple cider that would turn into vinegar. Ma had pickled vegetables from the garden. Pota- toes had been dug and stored, and corn was dried for hominy.

The dry peapods had been shelled. The root cellar was full of apples and pears from the orchard. The best pumpkins were stored in straw for Ma's pies. Hanging from the walls were bunches of wild sage, chicory, and peppermint that Ma would use for seasoning.

Samuel looked in and surveyed the bounty they would enjoy. He was saddened at the thought that Thomas would not enjoy the goodness like the rest of the family.

He had used a ladder to get up on the roof to check for shingles that needed to be replaced.

Ma kept calling out, "You be careful up there, son."

"I know this would be Thomas's job, but he is not here--so it's my job now," Samuel said.

Jenny helped when she was not taking care of little Thomas. The Blackwells had made their winter preparations as well. She did not stay at the cabin that much anymore, and she divided her time between the Blackwell and Lyle homes.

As Samuel was coming down the ladder from fixing the roof, he shouted, "Let winter come. We are ready for it."

"Hush talking like that," Ma said. "Winter is usually harsh enough without you talking like that. Bad things can happen, which we don't need."

Samuel carried the ladder to the tool shed and walked by Jenny. "The only bad thing right now is that Thomas is not here."

Jenny was playing with little Thomas on a quilt on the porch. She buried her face in her apron and began to sob.

"Samuel," Ma shouted as she rushed to console Jenny.

Samuel dropped the ladder, ran to the porch, and knelt down beside Jenny. "I am so sorry. I didn't say that to upset you."

After a few moments, Jenny stopped crying. She reached out to touch Samuel's arm. "I know you miss him too. I miss Thomas very, very much. I read some of his letters every day. I pray for hi safety. I want him to come home so very much." She pulled Samuel closer and gave him a hug. "I know you were not trying to make me sad. It is all right." She wiped her tears on her apron.

It took Samuel a few moments to recover.

Jenny began to play with little Thomas again, and Ma went back to her chores.

Samuel picked up the ladder and carried it to the work shed.

"I've got a letter," Pa called out when he returned from the general store. He had gone to the store to get salt for the hog killing. Ma wanted sugar and some other things, but there was no sugar. "We will use molasses to sweeten things," Ma said halfheartedly. "We will need to have a good sorghum cooking."

"Edward would only let me have a little salt." Pa placed the packages in Ma's outstretched hands. "I'll dig up some dirt from the smokehouse floor, and you can boil the salt from the dirt."

Pa said, "I am sorry, Jenny. I should have given this to you first."

"It's from Thomas!" Jenny sat down on the floor by little Thomas, carefully opened the letter, and began to read the mes- sage out loud:

My dearest jenny,

I have a few moments to write of recent events. I was in a hospital in Richmond} Virginia} in August. I had a fever off and on for several days. Our field doctor finally sent me to Saint Charles Hospital} which the army calls Hospital Number Eight.

Do you remember me writing about having to wade a swamp on one of our marches? The doctor thinks I might have caught something from slopping around in the swamp water.

I would have a fever for a few days} and then it would go away. For a day or two} I might not feel too badly. Then all of a sudden, I would get chills for about a day. Then the fever would come back. I am getting better. The chills and fevers are not as bad as they once were} and they are not happening as often as they once did.

It is now the first day of October. I know I should have written sooner because of the time it will take you to get this letter. Can you make me some more socks and a blanket? We have already had snow. Sometimes we have to wade rivers two or three feet deep. We were ordered to march to Romney. We had to leave so quickly we did not have time to load our provisions. We were told the wagons would follow.

It snowed on us all day and night while we marched. The snow was well above shoe top by the time we got to Romney. Our wagons did not arrive until the next afternoon. We had only the blankets we carried. Without axes, we could only gather sticks and brush for our fires.

I'm sorry I did not get a letter to you sooner. We have marched and marched all over northern Virginia. We have had several skirmishes with the Yankees. We pushed them to a river, and to get away from us} they walked on ice to get to the other side.

Write to me about what Thomas is doing. How big is he growing? Are you well? How is the rest of my family? How are your folks? We have heard that much of Tennessee is in Yankee control. With the fall of Henry and Donelson, I guess Clarksville is occupied. Has anything happened in Lone Oak? Tell everyone at church to keep praying for the war to end. I want to be home so very badly. I would even like to see the johnsons. I love you much and miss you.

Your devoted

Thomas

Jenny clutched the letter to her breast. When she looked up, tears were on her cheeks.

Ma put an arm around Jenny's shoulder and said, "We have a blanket and some clothes to make."

Jenny reached for little Thomas and hugged him until he began to squirm and fret.

Almeda sat down beside her and said, "I have been knitting a neck scarf for Thomas."

"Make some socks and a sweater too," Ma said. "Samuel, go to the smokehouse and bring me some molasses. John, get me some wood from the woodpile. I've got baking to do."

Chapter 24

The sun began to burn away a morning haze. The Confederates had the high ground. Before them were a sloping hillside, the Rappahannock River, and many lifeless blue clad bodies. The wounded who could not retreat across the river had spent a chilly night. Small fires behind the Confederate works had made the night bearable for the huddled occupants.

Both armies had been amassing for the first major battle of the 1863 spring. The Confederates were on the south side of the river, and the invading blue vermin were on the north riverbank. Every now and then, the Union forces would make a charge across their pontoon bridges. Most would not make it very far up the hillside before they joined those already prone on the ground.

While the Confederates reveled in their victories of turning back the Union advances, there was a somber mood to their actions. It was known that the war in the west was not going well. The Yankees had control of portions of the southern states. The jubilation of a small victory was dampened by the news of a lost battle elsewhere.

The Confederates had watched for several days the action across the river.

"It looks like we are about to have a little action," Will said. "They have set up a cannon across from us."

"It will be luck if they can put one anywhere close to us," Will said.

"Don't underestimate their ability." Thomas shielded his eyes from the morning sun. A moment later, the sound of horse hooves rapidly approaching garnered their attention.

The rider stopped near Thomas. "General Jackson has been notified of northern units to the west. We have been ordered to move westward immediately to shore up our defenses."

"Prepare to move out," shouted Thomas. "Gather your equipment. Send for the mules." The mules arrived and were hitched to the cannon and caisson that Thomas was supporting.

Thomas was set to give the order to fall in with the stream of troops already passing by their location. A cannon blast caused Thomas to look across the river. A white plume of smoke was floating upward from the cannon. The shell exploded short of their location.

"What did I tell you?" Will shouted with glee.

Will's words were answered with a second blast from a second cannon. Before he could blink an eye, an explosion sent dirt and wood splinters skyward only a few yards away.

Thomas was knocked from his feet. The blast sent him through the <u>air</u> for several yards. He landed against a tree. For a moment, he was able to stand, but his legs gave out, as he slowly slumped to the ground.

"Sergeant," Will called out. "Sergeant " Thomas groaned.

Will carefully straightened Thomas's body and attempted to wipe the dirt from his face.

"Come on, Will," someone shouted. "We are leaving. We've got to go."

"Okay, go on. I'll catch up," Will yelled above the sound of more cannon explosions. "I am not leaving Sergeant Lyle like this." Will pulled the canteen from Thomas's shoulder and offered him a sip. He dampened the cloth and wiped away more dirt. He found a gash on the side of Thomas's head and wrapped it with the wet cloth.

To hold the cloth in place, Will pulled Thomas's kepi down tight.

Thomas's right arm had an unusual crook to it, and his right leg was obviously broken.

Thomas whispered, "How bad is it, Will?"

Will replied, "You are going to be all right. I've got to go, but I'll send for help."

Thomas grabbed Will. "Look in my haversack and get the leather roll of Jenny's letters. Send them back to her... please."

"Hey, man, you are on your way home," Will said.

"No," Thomas said forcefully as he partially raised his head. Will paused for a moment and then reached for the haversack. He found the leather roll and stuffed it inside his shirt. "Thanks," Thomas said.

Will looked to the direction of the cannon blast, raised a fist, and shouted, "You Yankee bastards." He picked up his gear and ran to catch up with the others.

Thomas tried to move, but pain overtook him. He felt far worse than before. He tried to raise his head, but the motion caused pain and confusion. "Jenny, Abi... Abigail." He closed his eyes, and pictures of his farm and Abigail began to form. He tried to gain strength from the images, but they quickly faded. "Jenny," he struggled to repeat her name.

He wiped his brow and became aware of the pain in his arm and leg. He tried to look at his wounds, but his strength failed him. Darkness overtook him, and he lay motionless. Anyone passing by would have thought he was already dead.

Chapter 25

On a Saturday morning in the summer, Pa brought the wagon up from the stables. Ada and Molly, the Belgium horse pair, were harnessed in their finest for the Lyle family's trip to Clarksville.

Ma, Jenny, little Thomas, Almeda, and Samuel settled into the fresh hay on the wagon. Pa had loaded two bushels of roasting ears and a side of bacon to sell at the open-air market on the town square. Ma had a dozen eggs carefully nestled in her egg basket. She also was taking two hens for sale. Ma intended to take the money gained to get salt and sugar as well as cloth to make a shirt to send to Thomas.

Flour, salt, and sugar were in short supply. With the high demand, prices were very high. Pa had used the mill in the corn crib to grind corn into meal. When sugar was low, Ma used molasses from the sorghum crop. She had boiled salt from the smokehouse floor dirt, which was full of the grease dripping from the hams and bacon meat. With the few dollars she had saved and what they were carrying to sell, Ma hoped to get a little sugar and salt. She intended to use most of the money to buy cloth to make Thomas some shirts.

Though Clarksville was occupied by Federal troops, citizens could come and go to sell their wares and buy from local merchants. The Federal troops often tried to buy from the farmers, but no one wanted Union money.

The Lyles usually made the trip about once a month. Besides the buying and selling, the trip provided a way of obtaining information about the war from friends. Buying a local paper was not worth the price since the Union commander controlled what was printed, and no one wanted to read the Northern slant. It was better to get information from friends receiving letters from husbands and sons. Care had to be taken to avoid long conversations since the Federals were always watching.

The trip was uneventful, and everyone enjoyed the warm sunshine as they bounced on the soft hay. Little Thomas especially enjoyed being bounced and let out many giggles. He was beginning to walk, and he would stand with

Jenny's help until the wagon wheel hit a rut-and then he would fall down to bounce on the hay.

They rode the dusty road to the Cumberland River. Before boarding the ferry, they had to go through the Union checkpoint. Everyone had to get off the wagon. The soldiers stirred the hay with their bayonets and checked the baskets. Finding nothing, Pa was allowed to drive onto the ferry.

When they reached the public square, there was a large crowd in front on the hardware store. Some people were sobbing, and others looked dazed.

"What's happening?" Ma questioned.

Pa looked at Ma with a frightful expression. "It's not good whatever it is," he answered.

"There is a handbill posted on the store window." Samuel leaped to the ground and pushed his way through the crowd. He could not get close enough to read it, but someone told him it was the casualty list from a battle in Chancellorsville, Virginia.

Samuel retraced his steps to the wagon and reported what he had heard.

Pa stiffened, and Ma's face went ashen. Almeda covered her mouth with her hands. Jenny clutched little Thomas and had the most frightened look in the family.

Samuel went back to look at the list. People who found the names of their loved ones on the missing were bewildered as just how to take the news. Others were luckier.

"Thank God he's not on the list."

"Well, he's on the wounded list, but at least he's alive." Samuel finally found himself staring at the large poster.

Fear began to overtake him as he looked at the killed in action list. He ran his finger down the list of names: John Holcomb, Boyce Hyatt, Daniel Lewis, Harry Little, Robert Morton. "No Lyles," he shouted. Samuel's heart fluttered. "He's not on this list"

He moved to the next sheet with the names of the wounded. Samuel scanned the list, and relief settled over him. The third list provided information that canceled the feeling of relief. Samuel's eyes fell on the name he did not want to see. Thomas was on the missing list.

There it was. Thomas Hanner Lyle was on the missing list. All to other names seemed fuzzy, but Thomas's name was sharp and clear. Samuels' mind began to swirl. *Not killed ... not wounded ... but missing. Where is he? He could be missing and wounded.* Samuel prepared to take the information to the rest of the family.

"Excuse me."

Samuel turned and saw the looks of faces eager to learn the fate of loved ones. "He may not have been in that battle," someone said. Samuel heard others praying that they would not find the name they sought. He slowly made his way through the crowd and searched for the proper words to use. As he approached the wagon, Ma buried her face in her apron. Jenny clutched little Thomas.

"What did you find out?" Jenny asked anxiously.

Samuel answered before he climbed on board the wagon. "It's a casualty list from a battle in Chancellorsville, Virginia, which took place on May 1. Thomas's name is on the missing list —not on the wounded or killed list, but on the missing list."

Jenny began to sob, which scared little Thomas. Almeda put her arms around both of them.

Pa said, "Thomas may not have been in that battle. Imagine the confusion after a battle. Imagine the problems of getting everyone back into their companies. Thousands of men would be all mixed up. Why-"

Ma raised her hand. "Missing could still put him on the kill list."

"My Thomas is not dead," Jenny quickly said.

Samuel stood and said, "The list says that Thomas is missing. He could be in a different company or regiment and mixed up with different men. Hundreds, no thousands of men took place in the battle. There could be many reasons why he is on the missing list. At least his body was not found on the battlefield." Though he had tried to sound confident, Samuel had a sinking feeling. "Imagine the confusion in a hospital that is taking care of the wounded. If he were wounded, he could be in a hospital and simply be overlooked. We have lots of reasons to believe he's alive."

Ma lowered her apron. "He could be dead on the battlefield, and no one found him- or they could not recognize him and- "

"Stop it," Jenny shouted.

Little Thomas started to cry again.

"We have to believe that Thomas is alive. Yes, he could be overlooked in a hospital. He might be hurt and left behind as the battle moved to another location. He might have found help from someone. My Thomas- your Thomas- is alive."

"I am so sorry to have upset you Jenny," Ma said.

"I understand your feelings, Ma," Jenny said as she tried to calm little Thomas. "Until his name is on a list as killed, I have to believe he is still alive."

Pa said, "Let's go home and get away from this commotion. We can think about things better where it is quieter. Of course, we have to consider he is still alive. I don't feel like dickering over prices for what we brought to sell. We can come back another day."

After crossing the river, Pa looped the reins over the sideboard standard and put his arm around Ma. The horses plodded along the road unattended.

Almeda continued to console Jenny and help her with little Thomas.

Samuel was lost in his thoughts. He could not bear to think about never seeing Thomas again. It was still more than a year before he would be old enough to serve in the army. Regardless of his age, Ma would have much to say about that subject.

They rode on in silence. Ma rested her head on Pa's shoulder. Jenny clutched little Thomas. Almeda was tickling little Thomas's cheek with a piece of hay. A giggle brought a smile to Jenny's face, but her eyes did not smile.

Ma said, "I remember the day that Thomas was born. John, you were out in the back field planting corn. I was home alone. When the pains began, I started ringing the dinner bell. I went back to the kitchen to finish washing the dishes. I waited and waited, but you did not come. I rang the bell again and again. I was thinking I was going to have to do everything by myself until you finally showed up with Dr. Ross."

"I heard the bell," Pa said. "I was so excited. I just unhitched the horse and headed for Lone Oak to find the doctor. I could only think I needed to get to the doctor fast. I didn't think about coming to you first. I found him playing checkers at the store. I went busting in the door and yelled, 'It is time ' He just sat there and finished the game. I yelled, 'Hitch up your buggy.'" Pa turned to Ma. "He told me to calm down because there was plenty of time. Well, we did make it in time."

Almeda said, "I would have liked to have seen your faces when Bernice and I took your clothes that day."

"That was not funny to us," Samuel said as a slight smile parted his lips. "I have to confess. It was Thomas and me who stacked Zeke's wood. It was Thomas's idea, but I helped."

"Samuel, your ma and I thought you guys did it. You noticed we did not say anything. It did not hurt Zeke, and to tell the truth, we thought it was funny." Pa even managed a slight chuckle.

"I remember the day I first saw Thomas," Jenny said. "I thought he was a bit stuck up. Then there was the corn shucking. I don't know who was the most embarrassed- him or me. I remember the day he asked me to marry him. I remember his talk with my father and then leaving without seeing me. My family got a big laugh over that, but my family loves Thomas very much. He has taken very good care of me. I can't wait for him to come home and see little Thomas."

The rest of the trip was made in silence. Pa let everyone off at the house and drove the team of horses down to the stables. It was a most somber mood at the supper table.

As Jenny took little Thomas upstairs to bed, she said, "I know my Thomas is alive."

Chapter 26

Though the first October frost had occurred, it was a warm afternoon. Pa was leaving the general store when he was stopped by to see the postmaster, Mr. Able Harris. "John, I've got a pack- age for Jenny. Can you get it to her?"

"Sure, Able," Pa said as he took the package. "Is it from Thomas?"

"I don't know, John, but it is from Virginia-and it's addressed to Jenny."

Pa's hands began to tremble. If the package was from Thomas, then maybe it would prove that he was still alive. Why would Thomas be sending Jenny a package? "When was it mailed?" Pa asked.

Able had gone inside.

Pa would have normally taken his time getting home. Instead, he tapped Molly's rump with the reins and wasted no time. The wheels on the buggy hummed briskly as Molly broke into a trot.

It did not take long to cover the two miles to the farm. Pa took the road fork at the creek, which led to Thomas and Jenny's cabin. Jenny was rocking little Thomas on the porch. His stiff leg caused some difficulty, but he climbed down from the buggy as quickly as possible. "Jenny, I've got a package for you!"

"A package for me?" Jenny asked as she got up from her chair. "Who would be sending me a package?"

"I am not sure, but it is from Virginia."

Jenny nearly fell descending the porch steps. She handed little Thomas to Pa. "Is it from Thomas?"

"We ... uh, Able and I don't know."

"I wonder when it was mailed?" Her hands began to tremble as she looked at the brown paper and leather cords. She raised her head and looked at Pa. Neither spoke a word, but there was a message of hope between them.

Jenny returned to her chair and began to fumble with the leather knots.

Pa took out his pocketknife and cut one of the cords.

Jenny slipped the rest of the cords away and unfolded three layers of paper. Each layer brought a higher level of anticipation. As the last layer of paper was removed, their eyes fell upon a leather roll bound by a single cord. She tugged at the bowknot and unrolled the leather.

"These are letters I sent Thomas," she exclaimed.

One of the letters had a very noticeable bulge. There was no writing on the outside of the envelope. As Jenny opened the letter, a minie ball rolled into her hand. She could see that the letter was unfinished. "This must be the last letter he was writing to me," she said as she rolled the lead object around. "Why would he send me this?"

"It must have some special significance," Pa said. "I don't think Thomas would have collected a minie ball and send it to you unless it was special." Pa examined it and turned it over and over.

"Does this mean he was shot?" Jenny asked. They stared at the hideous object in her hand.

"If he was shot, he must still be alive if he could send this to me," Jenny said softly. "But why would he send these letters and not keep them close to himself?"

Pa did not know how to explain, but he could not help but believe she was right. If Thomas was alive, why didn't he keep the letters? Hope of Thomas being alive began to dim.

As Jenny gathered the letters together, tears swelled in her eyes. She's hurt at the thought that he might have been wounded. *Where and how bad he been hurt? Is he all right now?* Dozens of questions flooded her mind.

Hot tears trickled down her cheeks. She bound the letters and held out her arms to receive little Thomas.

"Are you alright?" Pa asked. Jenny nodded.

"Do you want Ma or Almeda to come over to stay with you

tonight?"

"I will be all right. They don't need to do that," she said slowly and softly. She just wanted to be alone.

"Remember we are just across the way," Pa said as he climbed onto the buggy. Although little Thomas had not begun to talk much, Jenny held him up to see his grandfather and wave goodbye. With a giggle, little Thomas said, "Bye, Poppy."

Pa was glad he had turned around so little Thomas and Jenny could not see the tears making their way down his cheeks. It was bad enough to lose a son, but it was worse to lose a husband and a father. He began to dread having to share the news and events with the rest of the family.

Jenny and little Thomas watched until the buggy was out of sight. Jenny carried the baby into the cabin and prepared him for his afternoon nap. After putting Thomas in his bed, Jenny sat down at the table, untied the leather cord, and unfolded the leather.

Each letter brought back the memories surrounding her at the time it was written. She had written about family matters, the birth of Thomas, the spring planting, the fall harvesting, and community and church events.

After reading the last letter, she went to the dresser and took out the letters she had received from Thomas. She placed all the letters together, folded the leather, and tied the bundle.

She placed the bundle in the dresser drawer and paused for a moment. The letters had given her hope that Thomas was alive.

Chapter 27

May gave way to an early summer. The Lyle family had no further news about Thomas. Jenny was still the most optimistic that he was alive. Ma often stopped in the middle of work to stare out the window. Pa and Almeda had totally given up hope for Thomas's return. Samuel would have hope one day and be in despair on another day.

Even Lady and Ada acted differently. Lady mostly lay on the back porch near the upstairs door. Ada did not perform for Samuel as she had done for Thomas. It wasn't fun to go to the swimming hole. At church, there was always a space in the family pew where Thomas would have been seated.

Jenny spent most of her time tending to and playing with little Thomas. She continued to write letters to Thomas and tell him about how little Thomas was growing and things about the farm. She secretly mailed the letters from Clarksville. If she mailed the letters from Lone Oak, Able would know. If Able knew, word would get back to Ma and Pa.

Every afternoon, Jenny would sit on the cabin porch and read at least one of the letters in the leather roll. Every day, she subjected herself to this routine. She began to experience strange feelings of euphoria. The feelings started out as a mild sensation, but they now had a firm grip on her. One afternoon, a strange occurrence happened.

Little Thomas was in his bed for his afternoon nap. Jenny went to the dresser, pulled open the drawer, and took out the leather roll. She went to the porch rocking chair, closed her eyes, and thought about Thomas.

She opened her eyes, untied the string, and took out a letter. As she pulled the page from the envelope, the minie ball rolled into her lap. She read the letter over and over. Picking up the object that had caused the family to wonder about its message, she stared at it for a moment. She clutched the lead object in her hand. Closing her eyes, she laid her head back on the rocking chair pillow. Images of Thomas began to swirl through her thoughts. She stopped rocking as the images and thoughts went deeper into her being.

After a few minutes, she opened her eyes and found herself staring at the porch ceiling. A dirt dauber was capping off a cell in the mud nest it was building. With a long sigh, she lowered her head and look out across the hayfield in front of the cabin.

Jenny stared blankly at the butterflies flitting from flower to flower. She did not hear the chirping of the field sparrows. She was so deep in her inner being that she almost missed the movement coming into view. Someone was walking along the field road. She could not make out who it was, but they were coming toward the cabin. *It must be Samuel coming to see if everyone was all right.*

Just as she was about to close her eyes, she sat up suddenly. She squinted and saw it was not Samuel. It was Thomas. "Thomas!" she shouted as she jumped to her feet.

The letters fell to the porch floor. "Thomas!" She ran toward the yard gate.

Lady lifted her head to see what the commotion was all about. As Jenny ran through the gate, Lady resumed her curled- up position in front of the door.

"I knew you were alive. I knew you would come back to me." Jenny sobbed as she started down the road. She repeated Thomas's name over and over as she ran toward him. She ran with all of the speed she could muster. She became more and more excited each time she called his name.

The bend of the road momentarily blocked her sight of Thomas. "I knew you would come back to me. I love you, I love you. I am so happy you are back. Hurry and let us get back to the cabin to see ... little Thomas."

She was past the road bend, and she should have been able to see Thomas. "Thomas, where are you?" She called out his name with urgency. Her spirits fell to despair. "Where are you, Thomas? We can play hide-and-seek some other time." Jenny searched for Thomas behind trees and in the thick bushes.

"Come on, Thomas. Show yourself " She ran from tree to tree, expecting to see him. "Thomas, don't make me wait any longer. Please come out." She was getting exhausted. Being out of breath only added to her bewilderment.

As she stood in the middle of the road, she began to spin around and around. *So many trees. Which one is he hiding be- hind?* She spun so fast that her dress billowed out. She was get- ting dizzy, but she continued to turn about. Her emotions were so disorganized. She did not see any belongings Thomas might have been carrying.

She looked toward the cabin, expecting to see Thomas. There was no one on the porch. She began to tremble and feel faint. Her legs gave out, and she slumped to the ground. She became thoroughly unattached to the surroundings and sat there until the sun began to set. When she walked back to the cabin, each step was accompanied by a whisper of Thomas's name.

She kept asking herself why Thomas would play such a trick on her. It was a mean, mean trick to play, and she was going to give him a piece of her mind when she caught up to him. The closer she got to get to the cabin, the slower her steps were. It took all of her strength to mount each step and to make her way to the rocker. As she sat down, she was mentally and physically spent.

The letters were scattered over the porch floor, but she just looked over the hayfield. Her eyes were focused on nothing in particular.

Lady looked up and moved closer to the rocking chair.

Chapter 28

Samuel, take the morning milk to Jenny and tell her I will have eggs for her tomorrow." Ma handed him a crock jar of fresh milk.

Samuel took the jar and started on the errand. The path through the woods would take him past the springhouse that he and Thomas had rebuilt.

When he reached the springhouse, he put the milk inside. He continued onward to see Jenny and little Thomas. When he reached the garden, he heard little Thomas crying. He paused for a moment to see that weeding and hoeing had not been done. There were some vegetables that needed picking. He wondered what Jenny had been doing.

Jenny had been coming to see Ma, and it had been several days since he had been to her cabin. As he turned his attention to the cabin, he was puzzled by the cries of little Thomas. He wondered why Jenny was not tending to him.

As he came around the end of the porch to get to the steps, he saw Jenny sitting in the rocking chair. "Good morning, Jenny." He was taken aback at what he saw.

Jenny was motionless and staring at something. She did not even acknowledge his presence.

Little Thomas let out another wail. Samuel looked toward the cabin door.

Jenny remained motionless.

Confusion overtook him as another cry came from the open door. He entered the cabin and approached little Thomas's bed. Thomas was standing and holding onto the bed post. His gown was wet. Samuel turned to see if Jenny had followed him inside.

She was still sitting in the rocking chair. He looked around the unkempt room.

He decided to change Thomas and take him to Ma. The process baffled him since he had never done it before. After stripping the wet clothes away, he was thoroughly confused at how to redress his giggling nephew. After several tries, Samuel gave up and wrapped Thomas in a dry blanket. He set Thomas on his shoulders and ducked through the doorway.

Jenny did not acknowledge their presence. Samuel was even more concerned about her condition. Descending the steps, he began a slow jog homeward. Ma would know what to do. Thomas giggled at the "horsey ride" his uncle had given him many times before.

Ma was finishing the morning dishes that had been stacked on the table by the kitchen window. She allowed herself a quick look out the window as she reached for another dish. "What in the world?"

Ma dropped the dishcloth into the dishwater and moved quickly to the back door. "What is wrong, Samuel?" She pushed open the screen door.

"I don't ... I don't know." He handed little Thomas to Ma and strained to get his breath. "As I got close to the cabin, I could hear Thomas crying. When I got to the porch, Jenny was just sitting in the rocking chair. She did not even say hello to me. Thomas was crying, and I found him in his bed. He was wet, and I tried to... well, you can see what I did not get done."

Ma took Thomas and started to bounce him on her knee. "I don't think he has been fed this morning," Samuel said.

"Well, we can do something about that." Ma went to the kitchen, made a sugar-butter biscuit, and sent Samuel to the springhouse for milk. A glass of milk was soon on the table, and a second biscuit was disappearing. "Talk to me, Samuel."

Samuel repeated some of what he had already said. He spoke again of the lifeless stare on Jenny's face and the messy cabin. The more he told Ma, the more Ma's face showed concern.

"And Jenny is just sitting on the porch?" Ma asked.

Samuel could only give a little nod. He was finding it more and more difficult to talk about what he had seen.

Ma got up, handed Thomas to Samuel, and disappeared into the front room. She came back with her carpetbag of her "necessary items."

"Keep Thomas here," Ma instructed as she tied on her bonnet.

Samuel followed her out the door and sat down on the top porch step.

Pa was coming from the stables and met Ma as she started across the yard. He asked what she was doing, but Ma just shook her head and waved him off as she passed.

When Pa reached the porch, Samuel saw the inquisitive look on his face. He knew that Almeda would be back from berry picking soon. He really only wanted to tell the story once, but the look on Pa's face told him that was not going to happen.

When Samuel: finished telling Pa the news, Pa took Thomas and began to walk around the yard. Samuel began to wander aimlessly around the yard. As he passed a flowerbed, he grabbed a fist of flowers and angrily twisted them from their stems. He threw them to the ground and sat down on the cistern platform.

Pa took off his hat and placed it on Thomas's head, which brought a giggle from Thomas.

Almeda returned with a bucket of blackberries. "Is Jenny here?" she asked.

Samuel shook his head. "What's wrong with you?" "Ask Pa."

When Pa and Almeda were: finished talking, Almeda took Thomas to the oak tree swing. It did not take long for Almeda to swing Thomas to sleep. Almeda took the sleeping bundle inside and put him on her bed.

The morning went by slowly. Pa took a hoe and went to the garden even though nothing really needed hoeing. Samuel took the ax from the tool shed and started chopping wood. Almeda sat in her bedroom with Thomas. The ticking of the mantel clock sounded like someone was hammering on an anvil.

Almeda went outside to tell Pa she was going to the Blackwells.

"Don't go yet," Pa said. "Wait until Ma gets back. We don't know what she has been able to accomplish."

Almeda sobbed and buried her head in her hands. "What can we do?"

"I'm going to the spring to get a bucket of water." Samuel removed a bucket from its hanging place on the porch column. The spring provided water when the cistern was low.

The uncertainty and waiting were causing wear on their nerves. Even Pa was shaken by the turmoil of the morning.

As Samuel set the water bucket in its usual place, Ma returned with Jenny. Jenny was walking with help from Ma, but she showed no interest in her surroundings. Jenny continued to stare ahead blankly. She did not seem to recognize Almeda even when Almeda stood almost face-to-face with her. Almeda had a chilling feeling that Jenny was looking through her- and even into the beyond.

Ma ushered Jenny into the front bedroom and made Jenny comfortable in the bed. They all went to the kitchen table and sat down.

Ma said, "I have heard that women sometimes have un- usual thoughts or feelings after having babies. Quite frankly, I had funny feelings after you were born." Ma glanced in Samuel's direction.

"But that is another story. Since Thomas is almost two years old, I don't think that is the problem. She has been reading Thomas's letters over and over. I think she misses him so much that she kind of saw him in a dream or something."

"Did she say anything?" Pa asked.

"The only thing I could understand was she kept saying, 'Where are you, Thomas?' and 'Don't play a mean trick on me.' When I picked up the letters, she wanted to take them from me. She really got fussy when I would not let her have them. I think she misses Thomas so much that she kind of saw him in a dream or something,"

"What are we going to do?" asked Almeda.

Ma said, "Pa, hitch up the buggy so we can go to the Black- wells. Almeda, stay here with Jenny and Thomas."

"But I don't know what to do. I... I... I'll be scared if she- ''

Ma said, "She is sleeping now. She is exhausted. She will probably sleep for a long time. Samuel, go to Lone Oak to find Dr. Ross."

Everyone got busy with their assignments. When Ma gave instructions, she expected action. Samuel grabbed a sausage biscuit from the pie safe and started out the door. Pa went down the hill to the stables and hitched the horse to the buggy.

Samuel went to the room over the hardware store where Dr. Ross had an office. The doctor was not there, but the next likely place was across the road at the general store. There was usually a group of men playing checkers or whittling on the porch. Dr. Ross was putting a bandage on Zeke Wilson's hand. Zeke had let his knife slip, which had produced a nasty cut.

Samuel whispered, "Ma needs you to come to the farm.

Something has happened to Jenny."

Dr. Ross quickly finished up with Zeke. "Go hitch up my buggy while I get my bag."

Samuel had the buggy ready by the time Dr. Ross made it to the stables. He climbed aboard, and Samuel handed over the reins. "What is going on with Jenny?"

Samuel summarized the events of the day as they made their way toward the farm.

By the time Samuel and the doctor arrived at the farm, Ma and Pa were back with the Blackwells. Everyone waited on the front porch while Ma, Jenny's mother, and Dr. Ross examined Jenny. The silence on the porch was deafening. No one spoke because no one could imagine what was going on in the bedroom.

Mr. Blackwell began to pace back and forth across the porch. He would pace for a while and then sit for a while. After nearly an hour, the ladies and Dr. Ross emerged.

Dr. Ross said, "I have never seen anything like this myself, but I have read about illnesses like this. Jenny has something called melancholia. She has experienced something that has put her mind in conflict with what she knows to be true. All those letters she read and how often she read them put the image of Thomas in her mind. All this time without hearing from Thomas sent the message that Thomas was probably dead. As she tries to deal with both of those ideas, she ... her mind cannot deal with the conflict. I know you families have been stressed by not knowing what has happened to Thomas. I know you have been supportive of Jenny, but the time she has spent alone has given her the opportunity to daydream about Thomas."

"How long will she be like this?" Mr. Blackwell asked. "It's... hard to say," Dr. Ross answered. "With patience and a lot of love and understanding from all of you, it could take two or three months- or it could take much longer. You will need to remove all the things that remind her of Thomas. I don't think she should be left alone."

"She can stay with us," both Ma and Mrs. Blackwell said together.

"We have her comfortable now. I don't think we should move her so soon." Dr. Ross looked at Mrs. Blackwell. "I know both families want the best for her. I know you will work together for her."

When Dr. Ross departed, everyone talked softly so their voices would not carry through the front window.

Mrs. Blackwell said, "I don't know how you folks have been able to handle not knowing whether Thomas is alive."

"It has caused a great deal of concern for us as well," added Mr. Blackwell.

"I will not deny that it has upset us," Ma responded. "We just hold onto hope that missing means he is alive." Ma knew that the statement was not exactly true, but she did not want to give the Blackwells the idea that there was doubt in the Lyle family.

The Blackwells stayed a while longer and discussed how they could help Jenny and little Thomas. As they stood to leave, Ma gave Alice a hug and said, "I know it must be heartbreaking to see Jenny this way."

Alice said, "James and I cannot imagine what it must be like for you and John."

As the Blackwells boarded their buggy, James placed his hand on John's shoulder. "At least we know where our daughter is. I cannot imagine how I would react if my son was missing." John nodded, and their eyes met. No other words needed to be spoken.

As the Blackwells disappeared down the hill, Ma sat on the swing.

Samuel told Almeda that everything was going to be all right and joined Pa in the stables for chores.

Almeda joined Ma on the front porch swing. They sat motionless for a while, and then Almeda went to her room.

Ma was left alone with her thoughts. She remembered the day John and Thomas met the new folks down at the creek. John had really liked the family. Thomas reported that they had a twelve- or thirteen-year-old pigtailed girl and two younger sisters. She chuckled at his emphasis of the term girl. That had been nearly eight years ago.

She remembered watching Jenny grow into a young lady with striking features, which Thomas eventually noticed. She saw Thomas as a little boy playing at the end of cornrows as she and John hoed the corn. She remembered chubby hands bringing weed flowers to her. She remembered the disappointment that Almeda was a girl as he cried that he did not get a brother.

With the evening chores completed, Pa and Samuel returned to the porch.

Almeda returned from her room, and Lady walked over to Samuel and held up a paw.

After Samuel gave her the attention she had been missing, Lady lay down beside him.

Ma said, "What are we going to do?"

Pa stood and said, "We are all in this together-you, me, James, Alice, their girls, Almeda, and Samuel."

"I know. I am sorry," Ma said. "All of us have got to get Jenny through this. We are family, and I know my family is hungry. It has been a long time since breakfast. I have a family to feed."

Chapter 29

For, nearly three weeks, Jenny remained in bed. She hardly moved at all.

Ma and Pa moved to Samuel and Thomas's old room, and Samuel slept in the cabin to care for things. Ma or Almeda fed Jenny, but she did not speak or show any interest in little Thomas. Jenny slept all day some days and was awake at night. Some nights, she slept some. Ma, Alice, and Almeda took turns sitting with her because Dr. Ross had said she should not be left alone.

The sense of helplessness grew in everyone. It was agonizing that no one knew what to do. They showed so much love and concern for Jenny. Some days seemed much longer than other days.

Jenny's mother and sisters would come for visits. They played with little Thomas, but Jenny did not seem to pay much attention. Jenny surprised her mother one day by raising up to offer a hug. After a short hug, Jenny returned to her cocoon of blankets.

Everyone was excited but cautious. Several days slipped by before Jenny showed any other signs of interest in her surroundings.

One day while Ma and Almeda were preparing apples for drying, Jenny appeared in the doorway. Ma was so startled she dropped her knife into the pan of peelings in her lap.

"Oh, Jenny." Almeda rushed to retrieve a chair for Jenny. Jenny slowly sat down without speaking. She seemed nervous and did not offer to help. As they resumed their work, Ma and Almeda tried to involve her in a conversation, but Jenny did not respond.

When all the apples were prepared, Ma placed them in the sun to dry.

Almeda put the peels and cores in a bucket for the pigs, and Jenny went back to bed.

Ma walked to the smokehouse where Samuel was cleaning the smokehouse saltboxes and stacking the dried hickory wood for the fall hog killing.

"Samuel," Ma said as she ducked under the door post, "go to the Blackwells to tell them Jenny got out of bed for a while!"

Jenny remained in bed during suppertime that night and did not want the lamp lit. She seemed to prefer the darkness.

In the morning, Jenny joined Ma as she was washing the dishes. Jenny sat down at the table. After a while, she picked up the drying cloth and dried some of the dishes. While she was doing this, Ma slipped out back and found Samuel. "Go tell Alice that Jenny is up!"

With the dishes all washed and dried, Ma told Jenny she was going to the garden to pick vegetables. Basket in hand, Ma made the trek to the garden. As she began to pick the tomatoes, she turned to look back to the house. She was pleasantly surprised to see Jenny watching her from the porch.

Samuel arrived, and Alice rushed to give Jenny a hug. Jenny did not refuse the gesture, but she did not encourage a long- lasting embrace. Ma ushered them to the front porch. Ma knew Jenny was a daughter-in-law, but she was a daughter first. Ma did not want anything to upset the relationship between the two families.

Alice and Jenny spent several hours together on the swing. There were short periods of conversation. When Jenny got tired, Alice suggested perhaps she should go to bed.

Without any comment, Jenny went inside and went to bed. Margaret was preparing the evening meal in the kitchen, and the two mothers embraced. Alice expressed gratitude for all the things the Lyle family was doing for Jenny.

As Alice left to go home, she paused at the bedroom door. Jenny had rolled the bedclothes around herself like a shell. Alice could not help but tear up.

Ma put her arm around Alice and whispered, "She is getting better."

Chapter 30

Ma checked on Jenny before the rest of the Lyle family was called to the table.

Jenny was asleep, and Ma returned to the kitchen to put the meal on the table.

As Pa finished the evening prayer, Jenny appeared in the kitchen doorway. Seeing little Thomas in Almeda's lap, she approached with outstretched arms. Almeda lifted Thomas up for her. Jenny embraced Thomas and clutched him tightly.

Samuel and Almeda made room for Jenny to sit down. Everyone was glad to see Jenny up, but they were not sure what to say. Jenny smiled at everyone and began to feed Thomas. At the conclusion of the meal, Jenny excused herself and took Thomas to the rocking chair in the front room.

The rest of the family soon joined Jenny.

Jenny said, "How long have I not been myself?"

"Don't fret about any of this," Ma said. "It is just something that has happened. You are getting better. All of us are here to help you get well. You have not done anything to be ashamed of."

Jenny was far from being completely well, but everyone was elated about her progress. It was the first time in three months that Jenny had taken the evening meal with the rest of the family.

Before going to bed, Jenny gave Thomas a bath. They heard Jenny laughing and Thomas giggling as he splashed in the water.

Jenny finished the bath, put Thomas to bed, and rejoined the rest of the family.

Ma was sewing a patch on Samuel's pants. Almeda was knitting a blanket for Thomas's bed. Pa was whittling on a long-handled spoon for cooking the sorghum to make molasses. The pile of shavings grew as Pa neared the completion of the task.

"Now don't you make a mess on my clean floor," Ma scolded. Ma knew however Pa always cleaned up his messes.

Samuel was splicing the pieces of a broken plow line together. Jenny watched for a while and then went to bed. Ma wished her a good night's sleep.

Each day seemed to bring Jenny closer to the Jenny every- one had known. Jenny remained with the Lyles for another week. She spent some time with her family, and Dr. Ross made visits to see Jenny. He expressed cautious pleasure at her progress.

The families began to prepare for the fall and winter. Jenny helped when she was told what to do. After several weeks, she took it upon herself to begin and finish tasks without being prompted.

Dr. Ross suggested it would be all right to visit the cabin if someone went along with her. She returned from first trip shaken, but she was able to put the past behind. Each successive trip to the cabin strengthened her mental capacity. Finally, Dr. Ross allowed her to spend the day there, but she returned to the family for the night.

The hot days of summer gave way to cool fall nights. The chilly fall days gave way to the snows of winter. Samuel made sure the cabin wood box was always full for Jenny. Either by horse or the buggy, Samuel carried Jenny and Thomas home with him or to the Blackwell house.

Trips to Clarksville often revealed news of the war. Samuel made sure he checked the casualty lists and rejoiced at not seeing Thomas's name on any of the killed or wounded lists. He always stared longer at the missing list. Thomas's name never appeared on any list. The news brought hope. The news brought despair. It was almost two years after receiving Thomas's letters, but

Jenny continued to hold onto hope that she would see Thomas again.

During the snowy nights, Jenny wondered if Thomas was warm and dry. At each meal, she prayed that he had food. She also prayed that the illness that put him in the hospital had not returned.

The cold winter days eventually gave way to the warmth of spring. News came of Lee's surrender in Virginia. The war ending filled everyone with hope. The outcome was not what many had wanted, but the carnage and destruction coming to an end brought hopes for better times.

Chapter 31

Spring plowing and planting brought hopes of a bountiful har- vest. Little Thomas was growing and walking everywhere. Jenny followed him around the yard as he chased butterflies visiting the blooming flowers.

Jenny had assumed the duties of keeping the cabin clean, cooking for herself and Thomas, and all the other things needed to make life normal. After doing the daily chores, Jenny would read or do needlework on the porch.

One afternoon, after getting Thomas in his bed for his nap, Jenny turned to survey the room. Her eyes fell on the top drawer of the chest where the letter roll had been placed. She had come to know the cause of her trouble. For the longest time, she stared at the drawer. One step followed by a second and then a third brought the letters from Thomas closer.

With shaking hands, she pulled the drawer open. Her eyes fell on the brown leather roll. She closed her eyes and closed her fingers around the only thing that could bring her closer to Thomas. She pulled the package, and its contents close to her breast. Her hands began to tremble as she clutched the roll of letters.

She made her way to the porch and sat in the rocking chair. For the longest time, she could only stare at the bundle. Her fin- gers finally found the cord binding the roll. She could feel her heart beating faster. She slowly pulled on the cord. The loops of the bow grew smaller, and with a final tug, the leather roll began to uncoil. Many of the letters were worn from the numerous times their contents had been removed.

Jenny closed her eyes and rested her head on the back of the rocker. She wanted to read the letters one more time, but she did not want to repeat the past several months. "I don't know what to do," she screamed.

Lady looked up at her mistress.

Jenny opened her eyes and looked down at what she held. The letter with the bulge caught her eye. She always had found that particular letter the most intriguing. She could only imagine the significance of the object the letter contained.

Still deciding if she should read the letter or not, she closed her eyes. When she finally opened her eyes, she looked across the hayfield. It was not as though she expected the field to give her an answer. She glanced at the field as she had done many times when Thomas was working.

Just as Jenny started to look down at her hands holding the folded paper and the object the letter contained, something caught her eye across the way. She saw movement coming out of the woods to the road winding along the edge of the field. Someone was walking toward the cabin.

She froze and closed her eyes tightly. "Please be gone when I look again." As she parted her eyelids to let in light, she saw what she hoped she would not see. "No... no, not again!" She gathered the letters, jumped up from the rocking chair, and started for the door. Lady followed her to the door, but the door was shut quickly.

With her back to the door, Jenny slid down to the floor. Her back was pressed hard on the door as if she were trying to keep what was outside from getting into her presence. The letters spilled from her apron, and the lead artifact rolled across the floor.

Jenny stared at the ball of lead as it came to rest. Was this something Thomas had found? Or was it ... Jenny tried to stop her thoughts. Had it found its way to Thomas's body? Had he been trying to tell her he had been wounded? The turmoil caused Jenny to slump over. She drew up her knees and wrapped her arms around them. She began to rock to and for as the horrid thought tumbled through her mind.

Lady stood by the closed door, raised a paw, and scratched at the door.

Jenny did not move to open the door to let Lady join her.

Lady returned to her spot by the rocking chair. Just as she was about to lie down, the movement on the road caught her attention. The figure with a slight limp continued toward the cabin.

Lady watched as the slowly walking figure came nearer. At once, up went her ears. With a bark and a wag of the tail, Lady jumped from the porch and started for the road to greet the traveler.

END

ABOUT THE AUTHOR

Philip Chadwick was a high school Biology and Chemistry teacher for 39 years. He then taught freshman level Biology and Anatomy and Physiology at Austin Peay State University for 9 years. He was involved with Civil War Re-enacting and storytelling events. A favorite story teller conducted a workshop in which he described how to "kill grandma." You kill grandma by not telling grandma stories. One generation or maybe two and no one knows anything about grandma. Chadwick knew he had a Civil War ancestor. He left a re-enactment event determined to not let his great-grand uncle Thomas Hanner Lyle "die." Chadwick grew up on his farm in the 1950's and 1960's close by to the farm on which Thomas had lived. Both farms had operated with mule drawn equipment. The Yankee Present began to grow out of remembrances of his farm life. Though separated by time, the author realizes he would have done many of the farm activities just as his great grand uncle would have done. Plowing behind a team of mules and working with farm animals gave the author an interesting insight into what the life of Thomas Hanner Lyle would have been...

www.ingramcontent.com/pod-product-compliance
Lightning Source LLC
LaVergne TN
LVHW040139080526
838202LV00042B/2960